STRINGS

1   chicken grease

2   left and right

3   playa playa

4   greatdayinthemornin

5   feel like makin love

6   the line

7   one mo gin

8   devil's pie

9   send it on

10   the root

11   untitled (how does it feel)

1

chicken grease

Adjusting the lapels of my blazer while *Between the Sheets* serenaded the master suite, I stood tall in front of an African graffiti textured accent mirror - a slight crack displayed in the corner. Never one to believe in that superstitious seven years of bad luck bullshit, I hadn't rush to replace it. Part of me felt there was a mystique to broken mirrors aesthetically, sorta like my favorite installation exhibit in Israel called the Hall of Broken Mirrors, or in my opinion anything by contemporary master glassmaker Simon Berger. Ever catch a sunset's reflection across shattered glass? Shit's mesmerizing. Ight take me for instance. What I saw when I stared deep in my reflection was a distorted image not yet clear. I also saw a brilliant nigga having his fuckin way. I'm tough on myself, nowhere close to conquering my goals so the distorted part was plausible. Though my reflection may evoke a couple things, it's not the most prominent thing that defines me. Your shell is obsolete, unimportant as the soul is the one on the journey. As my mom would say, *the soul matters most.* Sometimes you gotta break the mirror, the mold, the reflection, your comfort zone to obtain the truest tangible results. Sometimes you just gotta barge straight through that muthafukka, defying all odds like the way I burst into the fashion industry. Over my shoulder my captivating, appointed guest is gazing at me in the reflection, watching me psychoanalyze myself. Momentarily I had forgotten I wasn't alone. Never much need to get their names really so I call em *Jane Does.* This particular Jane Doe dimly resembled my ex, only finer. Pink lipstick stains graced her champagne flute, sushi and oysters gone alongside some Mr Chow and McCallan 18. A bottle of 1942 sat empty on a nearby table. Reapplying makeup, slipping on her little black dress she took her sweet time swaying and harmonizing. The melodies echoed throughout the room creating a butter smooth effect. She clearly enjoyed her time and as drained as I was, she deserved it. Beautiful voice on her too as she was giving Ron Isley a run for his money on the harmonies. Jane Doe was now strapping up her Dior stilettos as her pretty eyes darted back towards me. *What are you thinking about?* A question I've always hated. A doper bitch would know better. The five words oozed from her glossy lips as she obviously could sense her time was wrapping up and desired to stick around. Ignite a connection perhaps. Anything to shy away from the sand being almost at the bottom of the hourglass. Anything to deter from the reality that she's a sex worker, her career selection of choice no judgement and myself, well I'm just a client. Two things were happening simultaneously here. She noticed I was the nigga running all this shit and saw a window of an opportunity as I noticed she was prettier with my dick in her mouth.

"You a spy?"

"No not at all handsome. My mission is to please and relax you, yet you still seem so deep in thought." She smiled seductively recrossing her legs ensuring to remind me she wasn't wearing panties, a dance we'd already done an hour back.

"I'm thinking time is money."

Glancing down at my Richard Mille which read 8pm signifying the florist would be pulling up in the speedboat any minute now with fresh flowers aka new women aka Jane Does. Mumbling something under her breath, this woman whom I'd never see again finally decided to pick up her speed a bit. Sensing agitation, I double checked my miscellaneous account ensuring her disdain wasn't financial. She had indeed been paid. Interesting how quickly a grin transforms into a frown nowadays.

"You mind if I drop some jewels on you before you go? I'll make it brief. Do you know what Robert F Smith, David Steward, Oprah, Kanye, Michael Jordan, Jay-Z and Tyler Perry all have in common? Those are a few of our black billionaires. My name will be on that list in a few years. Have you heard of Kerby Jean-Raymond, Aurora James, Telfar Clemens, Romeo Hunte, Carly Cushnie, and LaQuan Smith? Those are a few of the richest black fashion designers and I'll soon be on that list as well. Heard of Jay Jaxon? Well he's a pioneering Black designer of French couture from the slums of New York like myself. Worked in esteemed Parisian fashion houses like Yves Saint Laurent and Christian Dior, creating both couture and ready-to-wear. Left his mark creating clothes for performers and singers such as Annie Lennox's suit for the 1984 Grammy Awards. Legendary shit, right? Well guess what I'm doing and it only took me three years to pull off? I'm designing Mike Epp's suit for his new Netflix special. Very close to being chosen to design Don Cheadle's suit for the Oscars. Next year, Tyler the Creator. Shit not to mention…"

"What's your point?"

Jane Doe interjected with an eyeroll as she could probably sense her flag salute brewing. My wisdom being cut short on my own yacht wasn't really the vibe I was going for nevertheless I didn't hold that against her. She's just sad she can't stay. She was attempting to use her body to catapult her into a bigger role in my life and it was sad to see. A verse from the profound poet Jay Z echoed through my mind. *Just because you got good head, I'ma break bread so you can be livin' it up? Shit I parts with nothin, y'all be frontin. Me give my heart to a woman? Not for nothin', never happen, I'll be forever mackin.* With one quick swipe, I zipped up my fly giving her one final glance over.

"No point, just business advice for your journey on ya way out. You're a professional throat goat and should up your price."

Silence. Astonishment coated her face as I exited the master suite of my twenty-million-dollar yacht, and how did I become a yacht owner in only four years of successful business you may ask? I won it at a five-man poker game. Best night of my life. Can't forget it. That night, four years ago, everyone at the table raised as one of the players had only his keys to his yacht left so he tossed it in the pot and low and behold, the person least likely to win won that shit. Me. I had acquired my yacht while still living in my tiny condo and in the spirit of wealth attracting wealth, in time I manifested my mansion. I could feel Jane Doe's eyes piercing the back of my head on the walkout. Her pretty ass could stay put and gleam over the rare Asian wood coating the walls crafted to replicate ripples of the ocean. The cream, soft furnishes and crisp structures providing a casual feel aligning symmetrical to our casual moment. My plunge tub with the Japanese waterspout and Italian leather plush sofas, rich art peppered all-around. Patterned marble details, behind us an Egyptian backsplash. Appreciate the fact that she was roaming the sea on a massive yacht on a Tuesday night. Marinate some wealth into her pores for the remainder of her stay - ten more minutes maximum. Furthering the conversation was redundant. If she were truly paying attention this very small, meaningless moment with me should've changed her life. I mean considering everything is energy and all.

I tossed back a drink and headed up my bubinga wooden staircase, scooping up a piece of barbeque chicken from off a nearby plate. Smudged my shirt mid-bite which was no biggie as there were carousels of button-down shirts sprinkled throughout each suite. Strolling past a shirt rack, I tossed my soiled shirt in the trash and simply reapplied my blazer. Fuck a shirt. My bezzled out Jesus-piece draped my bare chest and the breeze felt good on my eight-pack. My very reliable assistant Bianca brushed past me towards the suite I was exiting. An NDA and gift basket for my hired guest in her hand. A smirk on her face. She was amazing at organizing my miscellaneous accounts –i.e., my Jane Does. Two rounds of sex followed up with a flawless dick suck always mentally prepared me for my evening's festivities. Had some clientele stopping through in a few to discuss contract extensions and needed suits for some black-tie events, so it was business as usual. Tonight, champagne was flowing, cigars were being sifted and the money.....we won't even get into the money but tonight was a celebration. What were we celebrating exactly? Life. More specifically. Black wealth. Tonight's mild wind mixed with the ocean aroma and ripples of the sea had me feeling good and lucky. Strolling over towards the lower level of my yacht past the glowing onyx wet bar and fruit arrangements, my four business associates Lyle, Chuck, Omar and my best friend Markell were kicked back. All four of my guys dripped in my fashion house threads, Prince Apparel high-end suits. The starting fuckin five. Moving across this industry in a full court press, everyone in position precisely where they need to be. We moved in a manner they'd never seen coming, displaying all-out effort exerting pressure and disrupting any opposition in our field. It's about black excellence and in order to reach that, you've gotta go all out.

Starting at number two, my Shooting Guard Chuck…my guy. He deals with all the numbers. Sporting a deep chocolate tweed suit from last year's collection with a black turtleneck, four functional sleeve buttons traced his arms, double vented, cream accents. Brown exudes relaxation and comfort so while not being the life of the party, Chuck's suit tonight represented someone people could trust. Grounded. That's Chuck. The accountant of Prince Apparel. The only one in the crew with a mansion bigger than mine. Met him in grad school a while back but knew him from the Yonkers streets as he'd always been known as the numbers guy. Back in the day he would run the streets as his photographic memory and way with numbers would help him memorize license plates. Made a lot of money off that shit, many moons ago. Chuck being ten years older than us, didn't party often and our conversations usually only entailed business. Personal preference. Chuck plays the harp, has stakes in high-end wines and loves luxury cars. He's got plenty.

In the anchors of my front court are my next two snipers, the lawyers. They are my first line of defense. Power Forward for sure, seated closest to Chuck at five feet nine inches, long dreads, known for being a master storyteller who could keep a room buzzing, straight outta Detroit was Lyle. Sporting a three-piece ash grey windowpane suit with tiny specks, a fuchsia pop of color graced his pocket square. Solid tie, a left chest welt pocket and bronze marble buttons from this year's collection. Bezzled out watch, ring, chain, frozen wrist;

nothing to gaudy, everything precise. Uncompromising attention to detail, versatility, alongside other key factors made him an essential part of the team. I correlated grey with experience and Lyle was young, yet he knew his shit. Howard University graduate, Lyle had a thing for drones, the techy type. He's pro polygamy, having two wives which he cheats on anyway so, it's all Swahili for he does what the fuck he wants to do. Not to mention his six children all which were well taken care of - something he emphasizes. He never had baby mama drama. Ever. Something he also emphasizes. He called it the Bob Marley way. I call it the Nick Cannon way.

Alongside Lyle, standing tall at six foot six, born and raised in Houston was Omar. Centre for his height and domineering disposition. Dripped in a simple navy pinstriped suit jacket with a single button front closure, chest slit pocket with two side welt pockets. Prada shades, Levi jeans, a Richard Pryor tee and a cigar dripping from his lip. Omar was always laid back, a country boy who owned a small farm, six motorcycles, sported a body full of tattoos and co-owned a bowling alley in West Hollywood. O spoke three languages and was huge on abstinence. Known for taking a muthafukka's girl and giving her back, having her strung out straight off the vibe.

My number three following up a career season of consecutively getting the fuckin bag is Markell. I can put him anywhere in the lineup and he will get the job done. The most adaptable, clever, and lowkey illest sniper I'd ever known and I mean that in the best way. Last but never least, my best friend. Small Forward for his patience and methodical thinking. When it comes to defense he can destroy any opposition, not to mention always creates openings for the team. Definitely the threat. An olive-green three-piece suit dripped his body. Slim-fit, Italian cut, dovetail collar, double flap, double slit and a single button clasped his Bengal striped button-down. Five black buttons traced his vest. Mustard lapel, abstract tie. New exclusive, unreleased shit. On his head lay a wicker hat with a feather. I'd label him the creative monster and my business soulmate. The only one there from the very beginning. Markell was huge on charity work, having his toe in every black association there was. He had mentoring programs for the youth and gave back a lot to inner-city communities. It was important to him and that's why I label him the soul of Prince Apparel. The heartbeat. The visionary. Foster kid turned Rastafari, highly devoted to his wife Donyale, father of twin daughters (my God babies) and a dog named ShakaZulu. Project kids turned college dormmates. When my concepts get too abstract, he simplifies it bringing it down to human understanding and vice versa.

I'm at Point for sure, for obvious reasons. Very obvious reasons. I'm the court general. Simple and fuckin plain. In lamest terms, all decisions concerning this bag had to be filtered through me. Tonight's original look consisted of a pink blazer, blue pants, a black textured button-down underneath - color blocked to perfection, a vibe only a certain type of man can successfully pull off. In real time I was still shirtless. The lining on my blazers were so butter smooth on the skin, any shirt just gets in the way for real. Notch lapel with a two-button up front and a single vent in back, three exterior pockets, five interior pockets. Who am I? Well, I'm the RZA of all this shit. Once upon a time we were a couple of ambitious but broke dudes from the hood. Now we size people up based on whether their suits have hand-finished lapels or if they thought English footwear beats Italian. My team sported huge grins as I grabbed one of many bottles of Ace of Spades, organizing tonight's itinerary in my mind. Watching Omar slide Lyle a hundred-dollar bill, I walked closer towards my guys.

"I told you Prince never smiles on the fuckin boat. We can order a slew of East African goddesses to fly in on magic carpets, fly this fool around the world like Aladdin and blow him from sunrise to sunset and he'd *still* have that stoic look plastered across his face. Don't ever bet against me Omar." Lyle talked his shit.

"Whateva man. Prince's mind just be deeply engulfed in the money. He's gonna be smiling like Christmas morning once we touch that billion."

Omar blew out smoke circles from his Cohiba Montecristo Humidor while Lyle created a paper plane out the hundred-dollar bill and whisked it off into the dusk sky. The ongoing joke was that I kept an expressionless look on my face. Some say due to playing too much poker. Took it to another level to say I never smile on my own yacht. Ever. *Master Stoic. Ice Cold. Poker face. Comatose. Al Bundy. Tinman.* They had their theories alongside their nick names. Was considered unpredictable because people could never tell what I was thinking, though to me it always seemed clear – world domination. Some say I always looked high which is funny because I don't smoke at all. Been labeled mean and mysterious. Some women thought I looked like I always rather be elsewhere which I felt stemmed from their own insecurities. Been labeled sultry, stern, emotionless, sedated. The world had me all wrong, but I just sat back and enjoyed the circus. I'm a rational guy who doesn't operate off feelings and emotions, simple as that. In real-time, watching my team bet on me like a horse at a racetrack made me shake my head. They found it entertaining as I thought these rich muthafukkas had far too much time on their hands.

"Yall lil paper bag games' more important than this meeting we got in twenty minutes? Tighten up and Lyle quit calling my *floating kingdom* a fuckin boat. That shit breaks my heart."

I reached for a nearby strawberry and bit off a piece as we all just gazed up at my thirty-two-meter super yacht in unison. A moment of silence for the queen *Yoruba*. Loads of exterior space with lush interior and gold trim. Penthouse that unfolded on top of the entire deck. Infinity wine cellar. Spa pools with laser lighting and plenty of hot tubs peppered throughout. Blue velvet trim tracing the waterslide from the deck towards the sea. Cinema, helipad, gym. Semi-covered deck containing an outdoor bar with plush sun pads. Below us, the detachable submarine for water digging. My triple-level super yacht, one of my most prized investments, interior-designed by Lenny Kravitz himself.

"You on ya Jodeci shit? Ya shirt. What happened to the shirt Prince?" Chuck took back his gin with a grin.

"Pussy. Chicken. A lot happened to the shirt Chuck and again, worried about the wrong shit. Where ya head at Chuck?"

"Shit since I discovered that the world's richest person makes $2,489 a second which is $149,352 a minute which breaks down to $215,049,600 a day my mind's been strictly on these numbers."

"One hundred forty-nine thousand, three fifty-three." Markell remedied with a smirk.

"Yall in the mood to make this quick half a mill?" I skimmed the money team, grins coated their faces as dollar signs danced in their eyes.

"King Prince!" Markell dapped me up.

"King Markell." I reciprocated the love.

Devil's Pie by D'Angelo rippled through the spot creating a smooth effect, as victory was near. Leading my team towards the main saloon to prepare for our meeting, our guests pulled up on time. Chuck's numbers were spot on, Lyle allured them with the jokes, Markel and Omar tag teamed them with creative strategies while I sealed the deal. The meeting went well, they signed the contract and we sent them on their way satisfied. A normal day in the life. Discussing a little business before everyone got drunk, Markell did his usual, awaited his connect to pull up in the speedboat to drop off his weed. Lyle was fuckin around with his drones. A buffet of chicken, macaroni and cheese, greens, yams and cornbread sat on a nearby table. Nine captivating belly dancers pranced around, decoration style as I'd ordered along with my chef, masseuse and boat staff doing their respective jobs. Not to mention some female acquaintances. The five of us linked up twice monthly on my yacht to build, bond and bullshit. Forty-five minutes of business and a few hours of relaxation. Tonight's fun consisted mostly of gambling and shooting the shit. Some of the crew and women fucked with the jet skis for a bit and then dispersed into the cinema room to watch movies. Spotted Omar heading towards a spa pool to meditate. I lay low playing two chess games with Markell. Our usual. He went to go get a massage while I dipped off to do my own thing as the cool breeze on my skin felt peaceful. Thirty minutes later, I'm kicked back in my captain's quarter watching Lyle and some fine woman in a lime green thong bikini have a dance off out on the cockpit.

She bust into the robot while Lyle was doing the worm. Nigga clearly lost his mind so I pressed a nearby button triggering my intercom system.

"The worm? In a five-thousand-dollar supreme limited edition Prince Apparel three-piece tux? That's how you feelin?" I hiked, my voice echoing throughout the airwaves. "Fuck off my *boat* Lyle."

Lyle flipped me the bird, mid-worm continuing to dance and it was pure comedy. Finishing up one of many pieces of chicken, I kept my eyes on my team. Lyle, Chuck, Markell and Omar. The money team. The four men I trusted most. Shit, the only men I trusted period. La familia. The men handcrafted and handpicked by the universe to catapult me to wealth. I truly trusted these men and I also knew nothing was coincidence. Nothing. Let's call a spade a spade. Yeah, we are five black millionaires and truth was, Lyle and Omar needed me. That's why they were around me. I kept them wealthy. Chuck, shit to an extreme extent I needed him. He worked my books. We were business partners so in retrospect, we all needed each other. That's why the happiness of my crew was essential. The brotherhood too, it was important we remained tight. Seeing everyone in unison was just as exhilarating as the money acquired. Black excellence only. Markell, well he knew me best. Known him since we were young. Real young. I was shy and he was loud and he'd push me to get out of my own way and out of my twin brother's shadow. My real brother Bruce was obnoxiously popular back then due to sports so I was left in the wind. The real story is, we both were pretty athletic. I mean our dad was a pretty athletic guy so one can say it was genetics. My twin and I equally loved basketball. A severe knee injury killed my NBA dreams at the tender age of nine but Bruce sprouted on eventually becoming the best power forward in the state! He was nice. At a point he was the number two college prospect with high hopes of attending a D1 school. He was the poppin athlete and I was the C student so I was invisible for a while. Back then, Markell would pull me aside and insist I see my real potential. He always respected me and I always trusted him and long as I had Markell, the absence of my bro Bruce wasn't as felt. Bruce sold weed, following after my dad's footsteps and always had the dope whips. Always had the baddest bitches too but the streets swallowed him up quick. Shit he only had two real summers of true flexin for real. Two summers. Bruce had popularity back then so I was left in the wind. Guess he was playing the immediate game and I was playing the long game, keeping my head in my schoolwork. Back to Markell though. He introduced me to the game. I introduced him to the paper. Markell planted the seed and I watered that muthafukka into a multimillion-dollar enterprise.

We are a colorful bunch, not your typical quintet. For instance, I recall the night we locked in our first big deal. It happened around the time I was fuckin shorty on the roof (I forget which one), Markell was having his twin daughters, Chuck was at the office, Lyle was at the casino down ten bands and Omar was out in Texas on his farm. Remember the time we got our first bit of exposure too. Lyle's crackhead cousin got arrested in none other than an orange Prince Apparel tuxedo jacket – something he stole from Lyle's closet. He punches the officer in the face, runs laps around the car, even squeezes in a moonwalk before they tackled and sicked the dogs on him. Plastered across the news and social media, a dancing crackhead in a mean suit. The bad press had our suits lookin so good and that was our first speck of exposure. Some wild ghetto shit. I remember my first groupie experience too. Snow bunnies. Generous, attentive, nasty snow bunnies.

Voyage to Atlantis was playing now. A song my dad used to play back in the day on vinyl for my mother before he'd hit the streets to grind. She was his sweetheart. *I'll always come back to you.... I'll alllllllwaysss come back to you.* The Isley Brothers marinated the atmosphere as I looked towards the night sky. Navy, grey, dark maroon is what tonight's sky displayed. The intriguing colors, patterns and lines had me mildly inspired as a memory permeated my mental. A scarf. Yeah, a scarf. She had a scarf those exact colors. She loved that scarf. It was when I tossed back my next drink when I saw her. *Her.* The room became hot immediately. Sauna-like. Coming out of my blazer, I blinked a couple of times keeping it cool. Internally losing my fuckin mind. The cool oozed out my body as beads of sweat dripped from my forehead and brow. My palms were perspiring as sweat dripped from my temple down my cheeks, all of this triggered from a simple fuckin thought. I could feel my heartbeat throughout my fingertips as I clenched my fists. Pulsating, similar to a madman playing the congas. Baboom! Baboom! Baboom! Wild drummer, wild drummer. *Why can I feel my fuckin heartbeat pulsate throughout my body? What the fuck!* Lightning flashes rippled through me causing me to buckle a bit. I gripped a nearby table while the whole room became chopped and screwed amidst my internal spiral. My brain was short-circuiting, at least that's how I felt. God knows what I looked like during these episodes. Taking back another shot, I attempted to shake it off. Time. I breathed for a moment giving life, time. The only cure for this shit. Closing my eyes, I counted down from ten……... three….two….one. Then I opened my eyes as she was still fuckin there. Dark, waist-length hair, dark eyes, thick eyebrows, full lips…it was definitely her. Shaking my head to ensure I was seeing what I was truly seeing, I eventually said *fuck it* and walked over towards her. This is my shit, fuck it. Dripping my arms around her waist, I pulled my baby close. She exhaled as I moved her hair towards one side, exposing one shoulder. I kissed on her neck and she melted into me, her scent captivating and pretty but not quite…. Captivating and pretty but not quite…not quite, her. Blinking profusely, took about ten seconds to realize I was holding Maria, not my ex. Releasing her, I staggered back towards my captain's quarters to get a clearer view of my atmosphere. More importantly, get my mind together. Maria was still looking out into the ocean, used to my shit as I'd mistaken her for my ex many of times. It's the hair. To add insult to injury, Maria was three weeks pregnant with potentially my baby. Nothing like an unplanned pregnancy with a stranger to round out my impeccable portfolio. I slipped her a smooth quarter mill to do the smart thing yet she hadn't made any decisions to my knowledge. Couldn't even pinpoint to as when she got pregnant. Was it the back shots on the balcony or that time she fucked the shit outta me in between her shifts? Almost forgot about the time she put that bomb ass pussy on me in the jacuzzi. I mean, when does this bitch clean the yacht, my dick was consistently down her throat! Shit, was it even mine? Hos be lying so I couldn't call it. My phone made a noise interrupting my thoughts which implied that a hefty deposit had just dropped into my corporate account. 600,000 dollars. It was nice money, but I stayed unphased. That's how I always manifested more. 600K could always be a mill, a mill could always be three. Looking back towards Maria, she was now looking at me. Never could read her eyes. Guess that is what happens when you nut up in a woman you don't know. Shit, she's the key reason I tightened up with the NDAs. I flashed back to about a week ago when she told me she was pregnant. I shrugged, my natural reaction so she's cursing me out in Spanish and shit. I'm just blank staring the bitch because the truth is, I don't know her and she clearly didn't know me. That two hundred fifty grand calmed her down quick though. She's lucky she's *Selena fine*. Illest part is that although she *hated my guts*, deep down I knew she still wanted to slip me some pussy. She really wanted me to give a fuck about her.

Pretty lil dreamer. Maria was staring at me again with them unfamiliar eyes. Gazing down into the remnants of the remaining cognac left, in the reflection, *her* face again. I closed my eyes keeping still, reminding myself to breathe as the room was becoming hot again. The beginning of another one as I sat here completely exasperated from the last one! Not again. *Breathe Prince. Fuckin breathe.* Interrupted by a bang on the door, it was Markell.

"Prince! Open up."

I pushed a nearby button which unlocked the door for my boy. He just looked at me with that familiar look he gives me when he catches me drifting off.

"What up."

"You good? I saw you over there with Maria again. Ya mind right?" My best friend blew out weed smoke.

"Never better."

"I've watched you acquire millions strictly off your wit and discernment, yet you've potentially knocked up the help. My nigga, *she cleans the yacht!*"

"So what. I have everything under control."

"You sure? It's a time sensitive situation Prince."

"I'm aware and a part of your job description is to ensure I'm never slipping so I do respect your passion on the topic. Trust me."

"Touché. On that note, you gonna talk to Dr Swanson for real about the visions and stop pacifying it as anxiety?" Lisa Swanson was my therapist.

"When are you going to quit that cigaweed shit? You stinkin up the spot." My passive aggressive way of saying I was cool with discussing the topic furthermore. Markell smirked, enjoying his herb.

"I smell amazing. Better inquiry, we still got Hugo Boss in a headlock?" They were our direct competition in a deal at the time.

"Is a pig's pussy pork?"

"That's what they say. Oh yeah. The second round of women are on the way. I'm about to head home to the wife in a few."

"I'll be down in a minute."

"Righteous. Oh yea Prince. Last thing. I think it's in the bag. I can feel it." Markell referenced a huge award ceremony Prince Apparel had coming up. It was a big deal, so I had manifested simply getting nominated. Hadn't even thought about or even aspired to win. My mind was engulfed in other things. Not silly awards and their politics.

"If we do it'll be your manifestation, not mine. I map out we'll win in about two years." Chair reclined, I slipped out my hardbottoms and kicked my feet up.

"Nah we bust our ass. All them late nights?! We earned that shit. Deserve that shit."

Markell left a smoke trail as he went to join the crew. I reclined a bit more in my seat, turning on my favorite artist D'Angelo and let *Me and Those Dreaming Eyes of Mine* sift through the jumbo speakers. Stayed put for a while. Reflecting. Psychoanalyzing myself and everything around me. A plethora of questions. You ever analyze something to the degree where you can't grasp the difference between what's real or what you've created in your mind? Like the two worlds crossed wires somewhere. You ever imagined you'd acquire enough money to create whatever world you desired? All this money was symbolic to something that truly didn't appear on the surface. I just couldn't quite put my finger on it. False dichotomies. My money was simply a wall to prevent anyone from getting close to me. No one ever could get close to me. Only as close as I designed it. I'm self-aware enough to know that I have deep-rooted problems just like every human on this Earth. I'm just ill enough to ensure that one of em isn't money and what's the best way to pacify your problems? Get ya bread up. Then I started really thinking. Like really really thinking. Truth was, I didn't have a problem in the world. The world's filled with so many lazy, unlucky muthafukkas so I guess I feel guilty admitting it but I really am having my way out here. In real life. Me and my niggas. Fuck it. Who was I really fooling? I'm progressive, I'm rich and I'm black. I won a long time ago. I popped a molly and poured me another drink. Today was a good day.

2

left and right

*B*uzz *Buzz Buzzzzz.* I reached over towards my nightstand, hitting the snooze button on my alarm. Opening my eyes, the sunrays filtering through my vertical blinds distorted my view a bit. May have been last night's dosage. Took me a moment to adjust. I pray instantly as I always do, to see another day. Pray again for the chance to see another dollar. Then I text my mother a simple heart emoji and she sent one back. Our thing. Then I sent her flowers – water lilies, her favorite. Once my feet were placed on the floor, it was go time. Execution time. I hadn't acquired this wealth by being lazy. Imagine that. Nah, don't. I was off schedule but I was the king of the alleyoop, so I'd make up for it. God mode. My strict regimes and strong faith kept me intact. My dad's work ethic kept my wheels going and my momma's prayers kept me afloat. Candles burnt down to the stems, peace and harmony was the feng shui. I missed the sunrise due to my excessive night, but I gave myself a pass. Shit, last night's pussy was extra good - better yet, early morning. Threw my time off a bit. I usually averaged about three hours of sleep every night anyway. Had two business meetings both scheduled around whatever times I desired, alongside finalizing on some colors for my spring collection not to mention, a fashion show in a couple of weeks. My day, like most of my days, were butter smooth. Pressing a button, my glass doors opened allowing a gush of fresh air to swoosh into my room as I mapped out the essential tasks of my day. Strolling out towards my balcony, I hit up Markell.

"Prince!" Markell happened to be on his balcony as well, Versace robe and a cup of coffee in his hand, a newspaper in the other, an oversized Buddha statue hovered behind him.

"Markell. How you feelin about the fashion show?"

"Grand rising to you too brotha."

I let off a chuckle gazing off into the LA stratosphere. Echoes of Markell, Dr Swanson, a few women and even my momma, reminding me to *enjoy the moment* rippled volumes through my mental. "Grand rising."

"Fashion show is gonna be epic. I can feel it."

"It's gotta be. We gotta pull that shit off."

"We always do. Long as we don't overthink it."

"Last show was cool but we could do better."

"Cool? We got a standing ovation!"

"So what. That applause ain't shit and you know it. This time we get it right. Groundbreaking."

"Both the future and past are subservient to the present. Quit overthinking."

Before I could respond, Markell's wife Donnie slipped into the FaceTime frame sporting a matching robe, a blunt in her hand. She waved, kissed her husband and headed back inside. I chopped it up a bit with Markell and then got back to my regime.

Turning up *Cream* by the Wutang Clan, I increased my speed, now going full throttle on my treadmill. Four miles. My vintage Vladimir Kagan bed's Jack Lenor Larsen printed bedding dripped wildly onto the floor as housekeeping would be here soon to organize everything to my liking. Beads of sweat dripped from my pores as I embraced the pain. Closing my eyes while envisioning my next money moves, I Inhaled new beginnings and elevated currency. Exhaled excess baggage and dated thinking. Manifestation style. Everyday. Every morning. Two minutes later is when I got the call. It was my fine ass therapist Dr Swanson. I use the word therapist loosely. Heavy on the fine though. Pushing a button which connected my virtual session to the large monitor on my wall, I zoomed in on Lisa.

"You're early." Ambling across the room, I grabbed a white towel to wipe the sweat off my forehead and neck.

"You pushed your sessions up to eight remember? Good morning." Lisa Swanson slid her glasses onto her nose.

"I don't remember that. You have that in writing someplace? My assistant didn't tell me she received that confirmation." I watched my therapist avoid staring at my athletic body as I walked at a slow pace, cooling down.

"No, it was verbal. We can switch back to ten if that's best for you, but I remember you specifically saying to push our sessions up to eight. You're correct, I should have sent an email." I'd hit her with the minor details she'd missed, and she'd remain professional. That was our dance and she hid her agitation exquisitely.

"That won't be necessary. We're here now." I smirked a bit.

"Good. How have you been sleeping? Are you getting more than three hours in?"

"Got three and change last night."

"Okay good. What's going on with the women? Last session you called them your Achilles heel. Your vulnerable point."

"Nah I said I love women. That's your theory. Just because I have a massive sex drive and an array of options doesn't mean I have an issue."

"What have your last ten to fifteen situationships taught you?"

"What you mean?"

"You're the common denominator to the last twenty women you've slept with. You and only you, so what does all that say about you? What's your general consensus of the whole thing?"

"That I'm flexible."

"The casual orgies."

"What about em?" I reflected on some colorful times. Could even picture Lisa in some colorful positions.

"You called women *your release.*" Dr. Swanson read over her notes.

"I like that blouse. Accentuates your beautiful collar bone and neck. I love your neck. You have a really beautiful neck."

"Thank you but Prince, you can't say stuff like that."

"Damn, lemme find out you have deep-rooted issues with receiving compliments."

"Pardon?" Lisa's left eyebrow went up.

"Didn't mean to offend. I'm in fashion. You know that being my therapist and all. You know me more than anyone and you really do have a neck that would showcase high-end jewelry nicely. You truly do. I speak to everybody like that. It's all art to me but to make you more comfortable, I won't compliment you again." I didn't miss a beat, noticing she resembled an older Kimora Lee Simmons.

"Understood. Thank you." She cleaned her glasses. "Back to your sleeping patterns and speaking of triggers. I believe it stems from unresolved issues with your father's death."

"My dad being shot in the head in front of me a million years ago isn't affecting my sleeping patterns. It's just an emotional proximity. I was ten. He was in the streets. Reason why I have never been in the streets. That saved my life and I already discovered the silver lining to that tragedy long ago. Even spoke about it at Howard University last Spring. I think you need a better hypothesis because your approach is amateur." Slipping on a wife beater, I headed towards the mini kitchen off my room.

"Did my bringing up your father make you uncomfortable?"

"Nah."

"What about the blurred visions?"

"What about em?" Tossing carrots, goji berries, mango and leafy greens into a blender, I pushed *start*. Lisa just sighed.

"You still anti medication? I truly believe you are stressed and you cope with it by gambling, adrenaline filled activities and sex. The anxiety. Lack of sleep. I'm concerned Prince. You can easily become the wealthiest black man in the world which is great but what about your mental health?"

"Well since my mental health is your department, wouldn't that mean you failed?"

Dr Swanson sighed deep. "Prince. Are you even interested in switching up your routine a bit? Do you desire to make a change? Mr Roberson….Mr Roberson…."

"I'm listening to you, but if I seem a bit preoccupied don't mind me. I got some incredible sex this morning. Squirter." I downed my smoothie, looking deep into Dr Swanson's imploring eyes. "I mean, is this a safe space or nah? I'm feelin real judged." She was quiet, done with my shit clearly beginning to lose hope, so I opted to ease up and throw her a bone. "Alright. I apologize. You got me queen. It's my dad. I guess it's still haunting me." I bowed my head, pretending to be ashamed.

"I know it is. Finally, a breakthrough! Doesn't that feel good?" She'd become overly excited, like she cracked the da Vinci code or some shit. Like I was Matt Damon and she was Robin Williams and this was Good Will Hunting. It was cool seeing her smile though. This psychology shit was important to her.

"You're good Dr Swanson." I fed her some more bullshit – my usual. I play fair.

"Same time Thursday?"

"To bask in your brilliance and build with you? Absolutely." I licked my lips.

"Prince Roberson." Her eyes screamed, *cut the shit.*

"Lisa Swanson."

"That's our time."

I couldn't tell her about Sole'. Would never tell her about her. It wasn't her fuckin business. The only reason why I agreed to see Dr Swanson in the first place was because my sis Wanda Sykes was good friends with her and recommended it. Yes, I'm good friends with Wanda Sykes. I gamble with Adam Sandler, Shaq, Steve Harvey and Seal. Threw my second fashion house with Puffy a few years back. Jay Z and I respect each other's opinions. Whoopi Goldberg too. Samuel L Jackson was a mentor of mine. My circle was different. You see, my life wasn't normal. It was normal for me because I manifested it but to the average civilian – I was the shit and had everything under control. Not to mention, living the fuckin dream. They thought I was an industry plant unaware of the blood sweat and tears it took to get here. I called up Wanda, my usual after "therapy" sessions, to shoot the shit with her.

"What's up fool?"

"Morning black man. Get me off that jumbotron screen Prince." Wanda barked as I laughed, clicking her off the wall monitor. She was on set for a project.

"Done."

"When I call you, answer the phone regular. Don't have me plastered across no damn wall. You've got your speech ready?" Wanda referred to the award ceremony I kept vaguely forgetting about. I looked at all my prominently white events as minor steppingstones to catapult me to the next level. Nothing less, nothing more. Nothing deeper.

"I'm not winning that Wanda. If I do, I'll wing it…fuck it."

"Givenchy, Brioni, Armani and Tom Ford got you shook?" Those were the other nominees.

"They want me to tap dance for a plaque in exchange for my rights. I ain't conforming to Hollyweird. We good staying rich and indie over here."

"This is the business we chose. Gotta at least pretend to play ball."

"Fuck em all."

"You're impossible P. You still feeding Dr Swanson shit and labeling it sugar? I was told you're not making much progress. I told her to trade you out."

"Lisa told you that?"

"Dr Swanson did. Yeah."

"Well we can start with that being a HIPPA violation." I let out a chuckle. "Second, she'll never trade me out, she enjoys looking at me. Third, she's a terrible therapist and you're a bad friend for not telling her. Fuck her. Bitch is boring."

"She's your therapist not some potential pussy. She's allowed to be boring."

"It's all potential pussy and that therapist / patient shit is all foreplay to me. All of it. Lisa's probably masturbating to me right now and to keep it G, all she really wants to do is diversify her celebrity roster.

I see right through Lisa Swanson." I smoothed out my thick eyebrows.

"I'm still wrapping my head around you calling yourself a *celebrity*." Wanda hiked with a chuckle.

"You got jokes huh."

"You still putting your dick in every pussy that moves or you grew outta that?" Wanda popped her shit, big-sis style.

"Ya wife enjoy that potty mouth of yours?"

"How you think I got her?"

Wanda laughed as we both began discussing a lil business. Then she got off the phone with me for Kenya Barris. Wanda Sykes. Gotta love her. Instructing Alexa to play *Everybody Loves the Sunshine* by Roy Ayers as I smoothed out the vibe a bit. I crack my jokes, but I was laser focused so though I only had two meetings today, I still had shit to do. Checked some sports highlights and handled some money shit first. My barber stopped by for a quick shapeup and then we went to my chill room to fuck with the pool table. After he left I went to my gym to shoot some hoops solo, one of my favorite hobbies as these essential moments eased my mind. I had a team of thirty people anticipating my call for my meetings, which I planned on tackling after my afternoon run. Two hours later I was wrapping up meeting number one.

Conducted meeting number two while I was on the toilet. Real shit. After that I hit up Amber, a little friend I fuck from time to time. I was thinkin bout Lisa Swanson fine ass the whole time with Amber forreal. In and out with Amber and then I hit up my boy Superman aka Shaq.

"Shaq."

"Prince."

"Let's run it up."

"Meet me in Miami."

"Nah bro. Straight to Italy."

"Trust me. Pit stop, Miami."

"For what?"

"You'll see."

I didn't know what Shaq was talking about but I fueled up my jet anyway, preparing for the flyout. Before leaving the crib, Omar hit me summoning an emergency meeting so the starting five hopped on a quick zoom call. Omar was courtside at a basketball game, Lyle was at his daughter's cheerleading tournament, Chuck was in bed and Markell was kicked back in his zen garden smoking.

"Two words. Janelle Monae." Omar got straight to the point.

"You got Janelle?"

"Almost." Omar smiled referring to a big deal we were trying to lock down with the musician. Her brand was strictly suits so this was a big one. Huge.

"Stay on it Omar. Research what she likes, all of that. Butter her up. Queen treatment. The queen of queens. We need this one."

"I'll put my team on it. Enjoy the Lakers hosting the Celtics Omar." Markel puffed his trees.

"Good shit. Brothers. Kings. How's everyone feeling?" I commenced the quick meeting.

"Blessed."

"Peaceful and abundant."

"I'm watching my daughter flip, get to the point!" Lyle added obnoxiously, tunnel visioned on his baby's tournament.

"Why the other parents in the background got balloons and flowers?" I hiked on my boy.

"Now you know me better than that." Lyle altered the camera, displaying a bevy of balloons, gifts and flowers next to him. He didn't play about his kids.

"That dad shit looks lovely on you my boy! The fifty-grand will be there this afternoon. Chuck you on it?" I wrapped up Lyle's segment of the conversation as Chuck gave me the thumbs up. "Everyone's money is in route. The campaign about the billboard is Monday. Omar you still meeting with HBO?"

"Thursday afternoon."

"Good. Markell, brunch with Michael Rapaport. You going or should I send Bianca?"

"I'll put B on it."

You see, Omar and Lyle studied law and Markell ran the creative department but truth was we all did the same thing. We were snipers. Agents. Recruiters. Entrepreneurs. Sifting out the next segment, the next evolution, the next conduit to not only another bag but world domination. Chuck focused strictly on the numbers.

"Markell how's the gas?" My best friend was kicked back, eyes closed, high as a kite. His dog lay out next to him.

"I and I." Smoke circles sifted from his mouth.

"Chuck. Everything aligned?"

"Always." Chuck grinned, a redhead beside him in his bed wrapped in black sheets. He was clearly preoccupied.

"I'm out. Be safe. Peace." I wrapped up my mini meeting.

Two hours later I was on a private jet to Miami to go bullshit with my brother Shaq. When I landed he was putting the final touches on his Fun House event, a huge Superbowl preparty with carnival rides and dope performances. Shaq's jet had everything jumbo size customized to his oversized statuesque so when I hopped in my seat even though I'm six foot three, my legs dangled like a toddler. Shaq wasn't shit for this and he couldn't quit laughing. The next stop was supposed to be Prague to look at some vintage vehicles and gamble but in classic Shaq fashion, we rerouted.

"We're here."

"Where?"

"Here."

Looking out the window at my atmosphere at the Nevada desert and then back towards Shaq who was now tossing me a parachute, I shook my head.

"Should've fuckin known." I took back a drink as my big bro was now buckling himself up.

"It's time. Let's go."

"I signed up to flip some money and look at some vintage toys and kick it with some foreign women. You on one right now."

Shaq ignored me, walking towards the door of the jet as I grew hesitant. I was all for adrenaline-filled shit but this right here? Man I don't know. A million excuses circled my mental as why I'd rather the pilot just land this shit so I could go gamble already. I stayed put in my gradient two-piece linen suit, midnight blue faded out into grey. The board meeting in my mind was pointing towards telling Shaq he could jump solo, I'm good staying put but I could smell a sermon cooking. He wasn't letting me out of this one.

"You are about to become one of the wealthiest black fashion heads in the game and right now you're presented the opportunity to jump out of a jet in a Prince Apparel suit!! You telling me you're not going to cease this moment? Nah not you. Not Prince. Not my niggaaaaaa."

"You told me you never jumped out a plane yaself. How you trying to rev me up?" I rolled up my sleeves and strapped on the parachute spewing fake confidence, internally freaking out.

"I've jumped outta plenty of planes…...with a general."

"You ain't gonna pray or nothing huh. Just two niggas jumpin out a plane?"

"You're stalling asking too many questions. Let's go. Leap of faith time."

Four long minutes of deep contemplation elapsed before I snail walked towards the door taking my time, having a heart to heart with God for real. I hadn't planned to do this shit today. Finally, I was a few feet away from the door and was preparing the countdown. Goggles on my face. I was ready or at least as ready as I was going to be. If I died today I was going to kill Shaq, word up. It was now countdown time. One…......two…..........*Push*! A shove towards my back and I was floating in the sky like a feather in the wind. Above me about a story up, Shaq with a smile. Nothing but the world below me. My world if I wanted it and this was one of the most exhilarating experiences of my life. We landed safe and immediately hit the desert to ride sand dunes, an adrenaline-filled experience for off-road enthusiasts. Hopping on our Suzuki RM250s we were off zigzagging through the desert at elevated speeds. Mashing on the gas, I revved up my engine. Plateaus and views of the strip as my airconditioned helmet kept me cool. Looking out for drop-offs and *witch's eyes* along the way. A witch's eye is a deep hole that forms in the sand which vary widely in size. Most of the time they are at the backside of a dune and are very hard to see. A reason why you should never ride straight up a dune but instead, ride at an angle so that you can see oncoming riders and other obstacles like a witch's eye. Then we went drifting in Vegas at 100 miles an hour. Chilled with some women that night and the following day we were gambling in Prague for about thirty hours. Yeah it was like dat. I was heavily engulfed at the crap tables completely oblivious to time. Time is technically an illusion anyway. It's not real. The croupier kept smiling my way which ain't mean shit to me, as it was always money over pussy for me. Shaq was on the other side of the room running it up when I was at the tables up thirty-three grand when I looked towards my watch. Alerts out the ass as I'd almost forgotten about the fuckin award show!

"Shaq! Yo! Let's roll. I gotta go." He looked my way and we headed towards the exit to the jet.

"Relax you'll get back to LA on time. You'll be ight. Party don't start til Prince pop up right?"

"You making me late bro." I looked at my watch and then towards the night sky as Shaq let out a chuckle, shoes kicked off.

"I'm proud of you man. I remember when I first met you. Arrogant as shit."

"Confident man, *confident.*"

"There's a fine line. Microscopic."

"Touché."

"What I'm saying is I've witnessed your evolution. Your glow up. You've always been eager to learn. Always had the fire in your eye. Always knew the importance of getting into the right rooms and absorbing the knowledge. Never asked for a handout. Always worked for it. You're doing something right kid." Shit meant the world coming from my brother Shaq who I highly respected.

"Thanks man."

"….still a bitch for hesitating to jump out the plane though."

"You the biggest bitch for not having on a Prince Apparel suit on right muthafukkin now!"

We laughed our asses off as we watched the game on the way back to my jet. Always a flawless time with my boy! Always.

3

playa playa

I was jetlagged as shit fucking around with Shaq but I made it home in decent time. The clock read seven pm which equated to two hours away from the ceremony. You'd think I'd be rushing but I was taking my time. Partly because I couldn't quite decide on a suit. I had hundreds of suits floating around electric carousel garment racks ultimately choosing my top five, a five-way tie. Finally choosing my top three after some heavy contemplation, I ended up flipping a coin - the winning suit slingshotting me into memory lane. Flipped another coin on it, same suit. One more time and yeah, same result so I figured it was written. A destiny thing. It was Sole's design.

You see, back in college it was me, Sole' and Markell. That was Prince Apparel. Before that, just Markell and I. We adopted casually wearing suits. Rocking em to the local parties, cookouts, basketball games, everywhere - engraving it our signature thing. Being two kids from the projects, we made that shit distinct and fly. To take it even further back, my mother being huge in the church sent me and my brother Bruce to school in suits when we were in grade school. Weren't nice suits either. Ill-fitting Good Will, hand-me-down suits. I mean, we were dirt-poor so it was what it was. Originally, I hated being forced to wear that shit. In time I became fascinated with it, but it took me a while to get there. Used to think my mom was trying to destroy my reputation making me wear that shit to school. Markell snapped me outta that ignorance labelling my mom the angel of Prince Apparel and

Markell the conduit to the genius of our thriving business. Back in the day I would get teased for wearing church clothes but Markell would flip the script and tell people I dressed prestigious. Said I dressed like the president. This was before Obama. I went from being teased to finding a friend who had a little influence who thought it was dope. He came to my house one morning before school and during breakfast asked my mom if she could hook him up with some suits too and from there it was on. We were gliding through Yonkers like Shorty and Detroit Redd. Markell always laced his with one of my dad's hats. I found my voice after that - a pivotal moment. Now I'm running a multi-million-dollar business. Over time I realized that suits were elite. I mean, even the illest pimps and baddest preachers wore suits. The sharpest businessmen and women – suits. Respected Muslims, suits. Suits represented masculinity, excellence and authority. Not to mention there's nothing sexier than a woman in a pants suit. Sheesh! We had a dream which put itself together in retrospect. We would brainstorm and try to find investors for years to no avail until Sole' and her abstract connections changed the game. She connected the dots. Sole' was a genius in her own right but she was rebellious, so in true preacher's daughter fashion she sporadically danced at The Pearl, a gentlemen's club deep in the valley. There is how she linked up with some Arab heavy hitter who invited her to a high-end event at the museum with nothing but the best of the best investors. Big money. Back then we didn't have a dime or a name of our company, just a logo – a gold crown. We had a few name options we all liked but hadn't solidified anything. Some options were *Da Suits* and *Royal Wear*. Long story short, Markel, Sole' and I dispersed the night of the gala reading the room attempting to work our magic to find an investor. Shit this was our last hope because at that point I was ready to give the fuck up. That night was high pressure, I remember. Everyone dispersed their separate ways to cover more ground. The museum was huge so it was the only way. Sole' sported a navy suit jacket with a dark red lace cami underneath that evening. Markell and I, two different shades of grey. By happenstance, an hour later I ended up singlehandedly locking down the investor and she loved the name Prince Apparel before even knowing my name was Prince. That's how that came into fruition. When Sole' and I broke up the final time, she said she wanted nothing to do with any of it and she was gone in the wind. Even sent her one hundred bands when I first started making real money, but she sent that shit back. Did I mention I fucked the wheels off my investor? Daisy. Interesting times. To keep it raw, my dick solidified my impeccable 85/15 split and Daisy's three million and fabric connect to start up Prince Apparel and that's the story on that. Me and Markell carried on alleyooping and manifesting this sexy, luxurious lifestyle we are living today ultimately adding Omar, Lyle and Chuck to the repertoire but none of that really matters right now, let's focus in on tonight's suit. Sole' always had the most distinctive design ideas. Her attention to detail and special touch made Prince Apparel sexy back then. Staring in the mirror at the amazing choice, I studied myself. Couldn't help to remember back in college when she designed this joint. She was lay out naked sketching all night, this being one of the three drawings. Her heart was never in Prince Apparel, but she loved me and back then would do anything to see me win. That and creative bitches got the best pussy. Don't get excited. On a fucked up day we'd be in handcuffs because she's jealous and toxic, trashing my condo or I'm hiding under her bed because I'm a little off too but that's another story.

I called my driver and made my way towards the venue. Quick thirty minutes. Seated alongside my team, head on a swivel reading the room, I noticed Markell had a gleam in his eye filled with genuine hope that we would win this shit. I mean, I felt with hard work and dedication we could win in a year or two but tonight Armani had it in the bag. It was a no brainer. Even had bets going on that Armani would win. The room was filled with heavy hitters, moguls and models as I played it suave and sat back taking it all in.

"I'm happy we made it this far."

Lyle leaned in towards me, clearly having bets on Armani too. Guess he was thinking the same thing I was thinking. Not tonight. Markell's overactive imagination sometimes got away from him. Thank God he wasn't a gambler with that abstract imagination. Creatives. I was proud of myself and my team for making it in the building, nonetheless. Thirty minutes later, they began distributing awards. I knew the business, so my being privy, knew it was all politics. All of it. Me sitting here in seat 16A next to Lyle, Markell, Omar and Chuck was politics. They just needed black faces here. The winners were prechosen. This shit didn't mean a thing. Nothing. Me being here tonight meant everything though. They see us. Next year we will win and then Prince Apparel will be closer to the gold. It's all leverage. Closer to that real wealth. Being here tonight lets them know we on they asses though. They think we're just filler seats but that's where they had us fucked up. Just give us a second. Ultimately, I never lose. I never did. It's just not my thing. I'm just good like that. I manifested getting here and that's the win. Tonight, Armani was going to make me a ton of money with this win. Then I'd flip that three hundred fifty grand and let that bubble. I was so engulfed in thought that I didn't even notice my team going crazy and the entire audience clapping. I couldn't hear anything, but I could surely see. Blinked again and tapped back into my actuality. Prince Apparel had won! We won in a category where the odds were not in our favor one bit and it was a surreal feeling. I looked back towards Armani who looked surprised too. Chuck led the way towards the stage as we followed suit dressed to kill, five kings. Once we approached the podium my team looked towards me to take the lead and begin the speech, but I insisted they went first. Lyle began, followed by Markell, Omar and then Chuck. All four men did their thing and then I finally took center stage. The women went a little extra crazy for me, I'm going to keep it G. After they chilled, I began to wing my speech.

"I'm shocked." I cleared my throat taking my time, serenading the crowd. "Speechless. Just because I'm the realest I know, I had bets on Armani. An uncomfortable amount of money so this win is bittersweet." I looked directly in one of the cameras as the audience laughed their asses off at the honesty. "Jokes aside. I'm honored. First I want to thank my mother who forced me to wear suits when I was a young boy. I was forced into this. Being from the projects in Yonkers, I was originally teased over it. Real bad. My mom didn't care, she was adamant about it and I couldn't understand why. I despised her for it. Can you imagine? She said if I couldn't wear my suits in the name of the Lord with my head high and cope with a lil bullying, then I was no king and therefore no son of hers. No pressure, right? Thankful for my right-hand Markell for helping me see that suits were cool. Suits were enterprising. Back then he would say, *suits are presidential*. We were ten then. I didn't start believing him until I was twelve. Thankful for Lyle, Omar and Chuck. My super team. The mega team. When us five come together like Voltron, no one can fuck wit it. The quintet. Chuck, Mr Numbers. Lyle and Omar, yin and yang - snipers, untouchable and the meanest lawyers in the states, not just Los Angeles. Appreciate yall dedication and sacrifice. Markell, the heartbeat, the creative genius, the spirit. Back to my momma, the queen. Shit all our mommas. Most importantly…." I stopped as my heart began beating and I began to perspire. Blinked a bit and I saw her. Sole' sitting in a now empty audience. You could hear a pin drop as no one was there. No one but her. Just her, front and center. Her hair was wet and she was in underwear and a wife beater. My wife beater. She loved wearing my clothes years ago, especially my wife beaters. She was drenched. Sorta like the night in college we got locked out of our dorm because her impulsive crazy ass desired to fuck under the stars. It started raining as she grew frantic, searching for our dorm key to no avail. I remember not being able to stop staring at her that night. Junior year, the most enchanting creature with ten toes. I shook my head as she was still there in the audience smiling. Her mouth whispered *c'mon Prince baby. Breathe. Breathe.* She was coaching me through it as I couldn't speak. I blinked again as the audience was back in place and Sole' was gone. Thousands of faces and I didn't know how long I'd been gone. Blinked again, Sole' again. *I feel your energy too baby it's okay* was what she uttered in my direction. Go the fuck away! I blinked again. How long had I drift off? Looking towards my team, expressionless demeanors. Back into the audience while I wiped the sweat from my brow. Reminding myself to breathe. Sole' was there again sitting amidst the audience this time. *I forgive you for not thanking me baby. It's complicated. Trust me I know. Breathe baby. I hate to see you like this.* Not now please! I reminded myself to breathe. *My suit looks real good on you. We made them tacos that night, remember? Well, you made em. I cut the avocados. Now hurry up and make that lil speech so we can go somewhere and fuck.* She was grinding in her seat seductively as all eyes were on me. I needed to say something. Say something Prince. Was anybody seeing this shit? I blinked again. To my left, my team staring at me. Back to the audience, Sole' was there again mouthing *say something*. Spewing imaginary support. Ignore her Prince. Don't fumble this shit. Do not fumble this fuckin bag!! The money Prince! The fuckin money!!!The bag. As the king of the alleyoop, I snapped the fuck out of it. "I'm speechless. I'm shocked and clearly at a loss for words. I'm thankful to God. This is for the poor little snotnose brown kid from the slums with the genius and business savvy, yearning to take the crown from me because Prince Apparel is coming for it all. All of it." I scurried through it, dropped the mic and strolled towards the exit while the room went crazy. We walked off the stage to Rick Ross's *Hustlin* and it felt like we won the super bowl. Oh yeah, you can always automatically feel when the price goes up. Omar was rubbing his hands, Markell was smiling like it was Christmas morning, Lyle was dancing hyping up the crowd, oh yeah we were lit. Me and Chuck played it suave and I was proud as shit of my team. All the extra love, real and fake was oh so sweet too.

***

After that miraculous win Prince Apparel was everywhere! Prior deals I had to negotiate were suddenly being thrown my way. Billboards, commercials, plastered all over social media. Felt like the world was on our nuts which in my eyes equated to one thing and one thing only. The price was going up. My phones were ringing off the hook, yet I kept my composure. It's never good to get overly excited about these things. My head stayed on a swivel and though the extra exposure was cute, I was money focused. Once the money started ballooning, then I'd get excited. All I was receiving were a bunch of higher ups trying to buy me out. Well I did receive one call that did pique my interest for about five minutes. A prominent company wanted to buy me out for a half a billion. I let my team sift through the details and it didn't take long for Markell to spot things weren't aligned, particularly regarding the shares part of the contract. Markell dumped a bunch of weed on the document, calling it bullshit. Chopping it up with my team, I opted to take the meeting anyway for entertainment purposes only. They only allowed for me to bring one person with me which was funny. They thought that the less people I brought with me, the easier for them to control the narrative.

I walked into the board meeting with Markell in tow. The only reason why they were meeting me was because Prince Apparel had just won the award. I kept that in mind but didn't show it. We were the only two black faces in the room which wasn't a surprise. Peeping the expressions on their faces through the glass walls on the walk up, reading the room I see six white and two Asian men standing to their feet. An applause erupted. Smiles plastered across their faces; an expression I knew stemmed from bullshit and deception. Just wrapping up

The Autobiography of Malcolm X for the ninth time, I was fresh on they asses. The applause continued as we took our seats. A slight smirk was my reply. This board meeting was going to be entertaining but not nearly as gratifying as the board meeting in my mind. The circus of deception wasted no time. A question asked about having part ownership in my franchise came about two minutes in. That made me laugh but I internalized that emotion, remaining poised. Cooler than the other side of the pillow. A quote from one of my favorite sports anchors, Stuart Scott. They brought up altering the way I did business. That was funny as well, especially for the fact that they sought me out. I didn't call them. They brought up possibly swapping out the two lawyers of my crew, Lyle and Omar for their lawyers.

"My people aren't interchangeable. My people concrete. Carryon though. Expound."

I politely shut down Ralphie boy with the fucked-up toupee' with a nonthreatening smile. These muthafukkas were on a roll. That's when they brought up shares which agitated me a bit. Only because the numbers clearly didn't add up. That was offensive. Chuck had already crunched the numbers over and over enough for me to know that they were trying to lowball me. On top of that, Markell found a few discrepancies. That was his specialty, peeping the bullshit. I called it the eye of the tiger. Not only were they trying to take creative rights to the dope shit I created out the mud. Blood, sweat and tears. The cherry on the shit sundae was they were swinging 82% ownership their way. All for what? For me to have their "machine" behind me as they were oblivious to the fact that they were looking at a machine. Me, Prince Roberson. Skimming the perimeter of the room at the way they were dressed; my creative team would laugh at the audacity. In the long run, they were trying to bury me. Lyle and Omar already combed through the contracts. Chuck did the numbers and Markell oversaw all of it. We weren't wit it. Three minutes later we were getting up to leave the room, Markel and I. Contracts unsigned of course. Exiting out, one of the suits had more questions.

"How did you find the hole in that contract? How are you so confident in your data? Who's educating you?" Out of the numerous questions this is what he decides to ask me. Simple entitled muthafukka. I just pointed to myself.

"Me. Prince Roberson. You see, every day I look up at the morning sun right. Stare directly into that muthafukka exuding up all that energy and then I walk back into my multimillion-dollar mansion and look in the mirror, deep in my brown face and I…educate…me. That's my formula." I emphasized each word.

"Even if we alter the contract?"

Reaching for my briefcase and smoothing out my tie, I looked towards the opposition. "At this point, *especially* if you alter your contract."

"But Prince..."

"Look, I believe in cutting the head off a dragon and no means no Todd. Respect it. On another tip, here's my card in case you need a suit. You know I've got plenty."

I grinned walking out of the board meeting exuding the confidence of Django. I met Markell at his Bentley continental since he drove. He was quiet.

"What's up?"

"*You* found the hole in the contract?" He reiterated, referring to what I mentioned in the meeting.

"Don't tell me you're upset about the semantics of that racist fuckin meeting. You're more clever than that." My best friend kept silent. "Markell." I was truly shocked at my righthand whom I paid extremely well.

"Just ain't like you." Markell rolled a blunt.

"You want to be the face of the company? Is that what you're implying? I mean you're my man, one hundred grand. Speak to me if that's what you want and if you think that's best. You can run things and I can orchestrate from the shadows in the wing. However you want to do this. We get the same check. Our roles are interchangeable."

"Nah Prince, I don't want to be the face of the company."

"You sure? It's all the same dollar my nigga, I promise. We started this shit."

"I can't do what you do and you can't do what I do. Relax."

Markell shook his head as I tried not to come off defensive, but it was what it was. We'd known each other forever and had been arguing like that since I could remember. Never been mad at each other longer than five minutes though. No one was more invested in Prince Apparel than me and Markell - like two men who adopted a child. Cruising towards my spot coasting to some De La Soul, three red lights in I opted to apologize. The day was too beautiful not to.

"I respect you. I should have told them it was your ideal."

Markell just let out a smile which reassured it was no hard feelings. "It ain't that Prince. Donyale lost the baby and I guess I'm still in my feelings about it." Donyale was Markell's wife of four years.

"Damn. I'm sorry. Sis okay?"

"Yeah, she's alright. She's strong."

I watched my friend face a blunt as we drove up to my mansion. "We supposed to be celebrating so enough of this somber shit. This weekend is going to be a movie. You wit me?"

"Always am."

"Don't I know it king. Don't I know it."

I hopped out the Bentley fixing the cufflinks on my wrists. Prince Apparel had just won an award, the meeting went flawless and the price was going up. Yeah, tonight was going to be good. Making a few calls, I put some of my finishing touches on a fashion show we had coming up. Everything was in place except the video quality which should be a quick fix. This show had to be perfectly produced in its entirety so of course I had a team working vigorously on it. Now that the price was going up, we tripled the rate on everything. Gotta pay to play. This business was oversaturated for sure, but there wasn't a team in the universe quite like us. We gave you persona, finesse, shit we created the vibe. A vast and regal feel. Not just a suit line – we provided an experience. A certain Jena Sequa. An energy force – I mean, what do you expect from five black kings? We also had the highest quality fabric imported from India, Jamaica and Africa. I felt like a caveman with a lighter, ahead of the curve and I was grateful. Had a few clients scheduled for fittings for a wedding so I'd deal with that in a few days. Strolling past a picture of my mentor Virgil, I tackled the remainder of my day.

The next night we met at Chuck's to celebrate another suit debut. Mike Epps' Netflix special was plastered across all TVs, the comedian dripped down in custom Prince Apparel. Chuck's spot had the golf course, so we were out back most of the time bullshittin enjoying the night. He was also ten years our senior and the wealthiest, so he had his rich friends over and we were taking their money in a game of guts. At least I was. Easy. Chuck had models prancing around in negligee serving drinks and food as we enjoyed the pregame. Two redheads sat on his lap and was treatin him like the Brooklyn ol school playa he was. They were feeding him grapes and treatin him like Big Willie – shit all of us. We got drunk, crashed some golf carts, I won thirty eight grand at a guts game and called it a night. The next evening we would hit the city.

***

Lucille my red Ferrari California equipped with a retractable electronic rooftop with the smoke grey interior was out tonight. Moonlit ceiling depending on the vibe. Tonight it was blacked out. Markel drove his forest green Lamborghini in with the oakwood trim leather interior. We flipped a coin, Lucille won and we hopped in.

"You auditioning for a western later?" Glazing over Markell's cowboy hat, buckles, and custom-fringed suit as he filled his pipe with herbs beside me.

"I'm the best dressed muthafukka in the crew by a landslide. You just ain't getting it. Tonight's look is inspired by our next theme - *grunge tuxedo*. For all my unpolished, unsophisticated, unrefined people. Creative team is working on it. You lookin at me crazy now but watch, it's gonna go. Get Johnny Depp or Rosario Dawson to model it. Maybe Travis Barker."

"I don't know but I trust ya vision my nigga."

I laughed as I revved up the engine and dipped off into the night meeting up with the fellas. LA traffic was a bitch as usual but fuck it. Shit what's the rush right? The night was perfect, I was with my best friend and life was good. Tilting my seat back, I enjoyed the LA view.

"We're rewriting history. Think about it. Look at us. Look at our life. We're a long fuckin way from bologna sandwiches in Yonkers." I cracked open a redbull.

"We have no choice but to rewrite this shit. I mean, look at our history Prince. We from the gutter."

"True."

"Shit, look how they feed us information. We're taught that George Washington's dentures were wood, never that they were made from his slave's teeth. They teach us about the ghetto but we gotta search for info on

Black Wallstreet. The real information is hidden and it's raw and its gritty. The history isn't pretty."

"Put that weed out in Lucille bro. All you do is eat blunts and go on philosophy rants." I rolled down both windows, coughing a bit.

"Nah."

"Nah?" I raised my eyebrow.

"Yeah. Nah. I'm not." Markel kept smoking.

"The fuck. Why not?"

"Because I smoke in my Lambo all the time and my shit blows this shit out the water."

"Nigga you crazy. No it don't."

"Yeah it do."

"Man, call Chuck." I suggested who was the luxury vehicle guru.

"You call him." Markel shrugged, which I did. Markell was high on crack to think any of his cars beat Lucille.

"Where you at Chuck?"

"With this pretty angel. She looks like Ariel from the little mermaid. I'll meet yall at Donnie's later on." Donnie's was Markel's wife's afterhours restaurant with a live band and amazing late-night comedy and food.

"Yeah yeah that red head shit you love, I know. Speaking of red, which toy is better my bloody Ferrari or Markel's Lambo?"

"Stop Prince. You know that forest green is sick. C'mon. I'll see yall in a few." Chuck laughed and hung up as Markel smiled wide at the victory, high as gas.

"Fuck you and Chuck. You're washing my car." I shook my head while answering my other ringing phone. "Yo. Aight. Bet." Wrapped up my conversation with my assistant; quick money chat as Markell put on some Lil Baby and kicked back. Lyle pulled up in his matte eggplant Maserati Quattroporte and Omar, his volcano orange McLaren: the toys were indeed out. Resembling a scene off Fast and Furious, we pulled up to a popular spot named Glow. People weren't breaking their necks when our vehicles pulled up because we were amongst the elite. There were a lot of exotic vehicles out as well as women. The line was sick though which wasn't the vibe. Even the VIP line was crazy.

"Why we here when Donnie's is jumping right now? This place ain't even black-owned." Lyle yelled from his Maserati.

"We bought out three VIP sections here but you want to go straight to Donnie's?" I looked towards Markell.

"It's my wife's spot fool. Just was coming here to get two drinks with yall, then I was out. I miss my wife." Markel ashed his joint.

"What time is it?" Omar asked as if his McLaren 720S Spider didn't have the time displayed someplace.

"9:45."

"Shit gets lit round eleven but I can eat now." Omar grinned sipping coconut water. He loved the sticky wings and rum punch at Markel's wife's spot. I was a fan of the fish tacos which is why the chef who worked there also worked my high-end events on the yacht. Best in LA.

"Now everyone has the *genius* idea to go straight to Donnie's. We out." Lucille and Prince Apparel were in the wind, racing across town towards Donnie's. Lyle and Omar dispersed, and everyone pulled up within moments of each other. Chuck followed in fifteen minutes behind, pulling up his chromed-out Rolls Royce phantom.

Everyone in this business understood that the walk-in is essential. It can break or make a moment. Me and my guys were always sharp, clean and effortlessly smooth with it. We hiked behind the scenes but in public always poised and cool. After a quick step and repeat for optics, we were in. The neon fluorescent lights had our walk-in resembling a scene from the movie Belly. Lights. Smoke. Applause. They even started a slow clap for my dawgs and I'm just a lil dirty boy from Yonkers with a dream, a gift of gab and a dope team. Best part was, I got to win with my boys. Donnie immediately jumped into her husband Markell's arms like a scene outta the film the Notebook, kissing like newlyweds.

"Yall really gonna sit here and act like yall don't live together." Lyle hiked with a grin.

"Shut up Lyle."

Donnie spat giving us all hugs, an African printed dress paired with a red lip was her vibe tonight. I gave my sis a hug and then browsed the buffet of women sprinkled around me. Felt like I died and went to Wakanda Heaven and this here was the after party. Scanning the room, the businessman in me hadn't spotted enough Prince Apparel suits for my satisfaction which simply meant I needed to work harder. Besides all that, the crowd was alluring as shit. *Medication* by Damion Marley echoed through the spot as we coasted in, heading straight towards VIP to chop it up.

"Prince did that shit again. Speech was a lil shaky but he definitely secured that win." Omar raised his glass, proposing a toast.

"Ahh fuck all that sentimental shit right now. There are some beautiful women in the building. *Damn.* A lot of fuckin chocolate." I admired our surroundings. Head on a swivel noticing Chuck wasn't quite looking like himself yet on the phone he sounded like he was in Heaven. "What's up with you Chuck?"

"Don't want to talk about it." Chuck took back his drink.

"Shit we all family, I'll talk about it. This nigga thinks he's burning." Lyle blurted out obnoxiously.

"Weren't you just lay up with something twenty minutes ago? That quick?" Confusion coated Markell's face. Shit, mine too!

"Reason why I'm abstinent. These women don't deserve my dick. How you livin Chuck?" Omar followed up with disgust.

"Last thing I want to do is talk about this man's dick. That's first and foremost. Second, yall make too much money to not be handling your personal business." I lectured my boys, uncle-like trying hard to hide my smirk. "Last and most importantly, bruh you're rich! Buy some fuckin condoms!!" Chuck didn't laugh a bit, just kept drinking and shaking his head.

"Well, ain't that the pot calling the kettle black." Markell whispered in my direction, referring to my pregnancy slipup with Maria. *Keep forgetting about that bitch!*

"Chuck. Do better. Fuck it we may as well go back to congratulating me. To Prince Apparel. I love you muthafukkas. I couldn't do it without you. To more millions." We clinked glasses and the energy was smooth as Markell sat beside me in the VIP booth.

"So Prince. What's the next move? What's going on in that money-machine mind?"

Before I could respond to Markell, Omar began discussing business strategies regarding diversifying our portfolio alongside increasing money flow. We all began building on collaboration. Markell and Omar delved into talk on investments for solar in low income to middleclass neighborhoods. I chopped it up with Lyle about our future dream to purchase a football team. Then we stopped at the food level.

"Yall know Markell is the mastermind behind manifesting winning the award and the key point to us finessing the meeting? He deserves full credit. He deserves the accolades." I educated my team.

"Mastermind Markell strikes again." Lyle gave Markell dap.

"Nah, magician Markell." I adjusted my tie.

"Thanks Prince. It would've been fly if you had that same energy in the game, not just back here in the huddle for the playback." My boy pointed towards me with a grin.

"The truth comes out. So you *are* salty about the meeting with them crackers!? I thought you of all people grasped the concept of one band one sound. Unison."

"Admit it Prince. You're self-preserving. I still love ya."

"You're wrong Markell but I'll let you have it."

Markell finished his drink, swiftly joining in on Chuck's conversation effortlessly keeping it moving. Self-preserving? Markell had me all wrong. Shit, I was self-sacrificing if anything. Splitting everything five ways like Boys to Men! All I ever thought about was Prince Apparel and when I thought of Prince Apparel, I thought about my crew. The five fuckin heartbeats. The quintet. The tribe. Markell, Lyle, Omar, Chuck and myself. Most times, putting myself last! I didn't blame Markell though. He's my best friend but he wasn't in my head. He didn't know how I truly thought. Grabbing my phone, I immediately sent Markell an all-paid luxury Hawaii vacation for him and his family – Donyale, and his twin daughters. I waited for him to check his phone and when he did, he looked towards me as we walked off to chat real quick.

"This my gift for claiming my ideal in front of the suits but celebrating it amongst our inner circle?"

"That's because you're my true brother and the only one real enough to check me. You rather the Maldives over Hawaii?" Ensuring that my squad was content and happy was essential. Heard of happy wife, happy life? Mine was happy team, more green.

"Nah Donnie and the girls love Hawaii. Just gotta find time to take these vacations. Appreciate you bro."

We gave each other dap which solidified everything was all good. Past the bullshit. Upward and onward. Back to the money. I sent him to the Maldives too. Followed up with a Disney cruise for my nieces. Fuck it. We ball! We took back a few drinks at the bar, Ciroc VSOP with a twist of lime. Then everyone did their own thing. Markel was back at the bar quick though.

"Yo tell these niggas stop fuckin in my wife's establishment. Disgusting. Disgusting!"

Lyle, a few feet behind him buttoning his pants, stumbled back towards the bar. "Bro. Live a little Kells."

"Not at Donnie's." Markel took his shot back.

"Not at Donnie's Lyle. You know better, tighten up." I followed up as the crew strolled back towards the VIP for a moment to shoot the shit.

"Had this slut in a shishkabob in my wife's nice establishment." Markell vented, tossing hand sanitizer Lyle's way.

"My bad. I forgot you and Omar be on yall Honorable Elijah Muhammad shit. Conservative muthafukkas."

"Dick clean as nun pussy. Don't leave that part out when speaking on me." Omar indulged in his wings.

"Ight Farrakhan. This tall Avatar muthafukka Omar goes on a million dates with the baddest of the baddest for pure entertainment. Taking them to museums and temples and steakhouses and Tahitian Serengeti's and the Japanese Alps and to see the Eiffel Tower and shit and don't even be fuckin all of em! Sup wit dat?"

"Them women be crazy over O too. Call that fool the male Badu. Shit I tell my women to close their eyes and use their imaginations. Bitch we can be anywhere in the world."

"I get to know them on a spiritual and intellectual level before I become physical with em. Something yall know shit about."

"Nah nigga, I heard it's because you're into that tantric sex shit."

"I am." Omar pulled out a Cuban cigar with a smile.

"Fuck is that?"

"An ancient Indian practice that merges spirituality and sexuality, emphasizing the importance of intimacy. It's a practice you can do alone or with a partner."

"Omar get that Eric Benet shit outta here man. You killin my buzz."

"Man fuck all dat, Lyle I was two inches from punching you in your throat fixing ya shit with my wife less than fifty feet away. Nasty filthy fuck." A no-nonsense expression coated Markell's face.

"That part. You're out of order Lyle. Bottom line." I tossed back fish tacos, laughing at my boys.

"Nigga I'm young and exciting! I'm the spark in this bitch. The sizzle. I'm just celebrating. On the dirtbag tip, that's more Chuck with Prince coming in at a close second if we're keeping it all the way a hundred."

"Order all fucked up. Flip that shit around."

"Erroneous. I'm not going to let yall create the false narrative of me being the *dirtbag of Prince Apparel* with hot dick Chuck sitting right here next to me .... Sorry Chuck." Lyle patted Chuck on the back spewing fake sympathy.

"Fuck you Lyle, short fuck. After my food comes out I'm heading home. Yall giving me a migraine." Chuck grumpily prepared his exit.

"Bottom line, you're my numbers guy Chuck. Get some sleep and handle ya business in the morning. Nice and neat. Don't sweat it." I spewed affirmations towards my boy, walking him towards valet to grab his Phantom. Once Chuck was in the wind, I zoomed back in on the array of women.

VIP was cool but I felt too closed off from the regular folk, so I broke free from my guys to go mingle. Lyle floated off with shawty he had folded up from the bathroom and Markell was off dancing with his wife. Omar was stuffing his face as the amazing array of women were still pouring in. Shit even the women standing outside in the line were beautiful. Making way around Donnie's like a rook moving amidst the board, a plethora of beautiful faces coated the room. *Take Me Away* by Daniel Caesar saturated the room – melodies butter smooth. The lyrics echoed rivers through me. Many options all around, a normal day in the life. Still moving, head on a swivel, I saw her again. It was really her this time. Shaking my head, not beat for this Sole' mirage bullshit tonight. Not tonight. Kept it moving and there she was again. Froze up like a deer in headlights because this time we were locking eyes. Mustard colored linen body suit draped her body and her back exposed. Gold strappy sandals. Gold clutch. Complexion Trigueño. Stunning but fuck all that as there's a lot of pretty potentials here tonight. I kept that shit moving, used to these mind tirades. That's what I named them. Fuckin mind tirades. Blurring my past with my present. *Boom*, her again except now she's in forest green and now I know it's a mind tirade. The truth is in the details. Ignoring it all, I smoothed myself out and made my way back to the bar to get a round of white Hennessey. We're celebrating. Fuck it. I was on my bullshit tonight. As I chased my molly with a shot, I heard a voice simultaneously from both ears.

"I saw you watching me from across the room."

Immediately assuming it was Sole', it wasn't. Standing up to get a better view, I see….twins. Identical. From being in this industry, I detected an Argentinean accent and what I was looking at were two goddesses. The other twin had on the dark green. The one in orange had a mole on her lip, sorta like my ex. The other twin didn't have it and didn't look like Sole' so much. I was intrigued by her most and planned on eating her pussy for a while just to spite the other. The one in the orange,

I wanted my dick down her throat. That was my first stop. Yeah, I had plans for them and lucky them because I'm a rich ass nigga with the dick of a god. I was definitely on my bullshit tonight and was going to give them exactly what they were looking for. Their minds' blown.

"You know who I am?"

The twins nodded their heads in unison. "Congrats on your win sexy."

"I knew you'd win. All five of them sexy sis for real. All five." The twins grinned, showing love to Prince Apparel.

"Stay right here." I instructed heading across the room towards Markell, sifting through the crowd. "Yo these twins bad as fuck. Which one you want?" I whispered towards my boy. He followed up with a laugh.

"Prince, my brotha. You trying to fuck up my marriage?" It may have been the molly, but those words echoed like a muthafukka for some reason.

"Nah. We celebrating. We can do whatever we want. Wyl out. We rich! We won. Lyle's right, you do need to live a little man." He wasn't smiling as I was oblivious to offending him once again. First in the board meeting and now here at the club. Markell valued his marriage, taking his union seriously. Managing a marriage to its entirety was high on his list. Family was essential to him and breaking generational curses, even more important. Spiritually we were in the same boat, so I understood his perspective except the only words that spewed from my inebriated face were, *Damn I'm lit.*

"Ight bro. I'm going home to my kids and dog. Get some water in you."

Markell dispersed out into the crowd, making his way out. That's the way he usually handled me when I got too lit. He'd just leave and hit me in the morning once I sobered up. He gave everyone dap and headed towards the exit. It's simple, he's a family man and I'm single. Fuck you really want from me? Watching my boy leave Donnie's, probably to do some dad stuff, I searched for the host. Quickly finding her, I asked for the microphone as she kindly obliged.

"Everyone I need your attention. Not to interrupt ya fun, I just want to say something real quick." A few women started *oooin* and *ahhin* from the crowd. Regular shit. "I want to present a toast to my business partner Markell Livingston. The husband of the owner of where we're at this evening, as yall know. Donnie's husband. My best friend. I wouldn't be shit if it weren't for him and that's the truth. The head of Prince Apparels' creative department. My right hand. The only man smarter than me and that's why I fucks with him. Thank you for your knowledge and wisdom and tolerance, my brotha. Raise yall glasses." I instructed as the crowd followed suit. Markell stood by the exit door, shaking his head with a grin. They put the spotlight on my boy and passed him the mic as he played it modest.

"Prince Apparel!" He raised his black fist, militant style in the air. The crowd repeated after him yelling *Prince Apparel!* "I love you Donnie. Makes ure you all tip these lovely waitresses and bartenders, and everybody..... drinks on Prince." Markell wrapped up his exit with a peace sign and a smile. Then he broke out as the party continued on.

I bought out the bar real quick, then took back my shot. My focus was now on what to do with these twins. Better yet my Trigueño duo from Argentina who were obediently waiting where I left them.

"Yall bored?" Both twins nodded their heads in unison. "Yall horny?" Heads were sill nodding. Shit, one twin was now glowing, wiggling like she had to pee she was so excited. "Let's go to Vegas."

An hour later we were boarding my helicopter to go to Vegas to gamble for a couple hours. I won a quarter million at a private poker game at the Bellagio which made me smile. Then I flew the twins out to the Poconos to ski and get my dick sucked. In route, I deposited $10,000 a piece into each of my four business associates accounts. The remainder into my mom's offshore account. Lucia and Valentina showed me a great time. A perfect choice for the *fly out*. I hit that pussy in Cali, Vegas and the Poconos and yes, each time felt different. They signed their NDAs and were on their way and that's just how things went that night.

4

greatdayinthemornin

Waking up beside one of the twins, my watch read ten o'clock equating to my being late to go see my mother! *Fuck!!* I hopped up, tossed on clothes and called my driver. Thirty minutes later I was in route to New York to see my mom. The twins' transportation was all set for them to do whatever alongside copies of their NDAs. I was still high from last night's dosage so I was tossing back Gatorade to sober up. Once monthly I accompanied my mother to church, so my being late wasn't something light. It was borderline unacceptable. Pulling up around noon, the Jaguar I bought her last spring was parked in the driveway; beside it her BMW. Yes I was a millionaire but my mom loved her original home so I lavished her in other ways. My mother was the only woman I never wanted to disappoint.

"Hey ma." I smiled once she answered the door. *I Am* by Cee Cee Winans' floated throughout her foyer.

"You're late." A stern look coated her face.

"We won the award ma."

"I watched it on tv. Good for you and the guys. You earned it, now about you being late to church." She wasn't letting up. Standing in the doorway, my smile remained as she finally smiled back, embracing me with a warm hug. She could never stay mad at me. I was forever her baby.

"I'm sorry ma."

"It's okay Prince. It's ok." She rubbed my back. The scent of blueberry muffins brewed from the kitchen. My first stop. "Pastor Kingston was preaching her tale off today, son. You missed a good one."

"I got caught up with business ma. You know how it is with me." I indulged in my mom's blueberry muffins with some hot chocolate.

"Mmm hmm. Business or with some women business?"

I just smiled focusing on the Price is Right plastered across my mother's 72-inch television. "I love you ma."

"I love you too son. I'll text you my church notes. Don't fly the helicopter in anymore, ok? Disturbs my neighbors." My mom passed me a piece of paper.

"I didn't. What's this?"

Skimming the document, my heart almost stopped when I read it. I looked at my mother, then back to the paper. *Cancer free.* The words seemed to pop off the paper. Cancer free. Cancer free. Cancer free! I looked towards my mother; tears weld up in my eyes. My mom had been battling cancer for a while now and had been keeping it low. Didn't even want to talk about it so I financially set her up to get in touch with the highest quality doctors the universe had. Three months later, today, she's telling me that she's cancer free! I hopped up and hugged my mom so tight. That day was the day I knew God was real.

"I'm so happy baby."

"Ma. *I'm* so happy." I looked at my mother through new eyes. The strongest woman I knew.

"Don't make it a big deal. Ain't no thang to a praying woman like myself." My mom winked, brushing off her shoulders like a playa.

"Obstacle slayer." I dried my eyes, playing it cool.

"Prayer warrior. That's me." My mom smiled wide. Pearls in each ear and draped across her neck. An oversized church hat graced her crown. A queen. My mom changed the channel to Die Hard as I kicked back in the recliner. Then she began putting her turkey wings in the oven. After that we watched the movie. At least attempted as I became distracted by a polaroid I hadn't seen in years of me and Sole'.

"Ma trash that picture."

"What picture?" She asked as I pointed towards exhibit A. "Never. She's a sweet girl. Just because you two weren't mature enough to get it right doesn't mean anything to me. She sends me a Christmas card every year ya know?"

"Nah, I didn't know." I was now skimming through other photos from the past. College days, me and Bruce, my dad. Memory lane like a muthafukka.

"Yall would've made some pretty babies." My mom was clearly in her bag today. Before I could respond my phone rang and it was Chuck.

"Chuck. I'm with my mom. What's up?"

"Tell her I said hello. I'm getting married man."

I just stood there for a moment, ensuring I was intaking the information properly. "Married?"

"Who's getting married?" My mom interrupted my conversation.

"Chuck." I uttered, still a bit dumbfounded. "Nigga, we'll talk about this later ight?" I hung up.

"Watch your language and *congratulations Chuck*." My momma sang melodically from the sofa. This nigga done went from the old head of the group with the fetish for redheads, to needing an antibiotic to a whole marriage. What in the midlife crisis? Fuck was wrong with this man? That muthafukkin Chuck. "Why you against Chuck finding love and getting married?" My mom interrupted my thoughts.

"Chuck's not in love ma."

"How do you know?"

"I don't care what he does personally but he's my accountant and I need him laser focused. It's all relative."

"Everyone's settling down son. I know you're young and you're rich and you're ambitious and handsome and all that beautiful stuff but c'mon. The only women you trust is me and your assistant and that's strictly business. You never get lonely?"

"Some of the loneliest people are in these disingenuous marriages."

"That's true."

"Why do people want me to adopt the theory that I have an issue? I don't see anyone commending me for my strict regimes, dedication and work ethic. Like my accolades are invisible. Why can't I be right and the world wrong?"

"I don't think you have a problem son. Carried you for nine months, I think you're perfect. Proud of you, you know that."

"I know."

"I just need you to consistently deal with yourself as an individual worthy of respect and make the world follow suit." My mom smiled her warm smile. "Just put God first."

"I do ma."

"Well do it more. Be happy for Chuck too."

"Hate to break your heart but Chuck's promiscuous ma. Chuck and Lyle are hos."

"Chuck, Lyle and you. Why do you exclude yourself from that list?" My mom began sifting through her knitting kit.

"I'm a ho, I'll own that. I'm careful though. My point isn't who's a ho and who isn't. My point is a ho should not be marrying a stranger especially when that ho is worth a couple million. He's signing contracts off an impulse working off feelings and emotions. And that ho oversees my books? Am I the only one seeing the endless red flags?" My mom just began knitting and indulging in the movie, tuning out my shit. She was fresh out of church and clearly didn't wanna hear all that. I glazed back over towards the photograph.

"Why you love Sole' so much ma?"

"Why *you* love Sole' so much, son?" My mom countered, mocking me with an innocent grin. I ignored her and focused back in on the movie. "We all need love son. All of us." My mom glanced towards a photograph of my father for a moment, then back to the tv. His murder was hard on her.

"True. That's why I have you queen."

"Son, stop being a ho. That's not noble and I don't ask for much so do that for your momma. How's my Markell? His family?"

"He's good mom. They're good."

"Those beautiful daughters and that lovely wife."

"Ma. Cut ties with my ex." I kept my eyes glued to the television.

"Okay. Only if you do one thing for me." My mom refuted as she poured creamer into her Obama coffee mug.

"Should've been a lawyer the way you negotiate." I loved my mom so whatever she was requesting, she could get twice.

***

Before I went to go find my brother to give him the news in person about our mother beating cancer, her intricate request, I had some business to handle so stopping through Yonkers was cool with me. I went through a few projects to handle a bit of marketing business for Prince Apparel. I had sixty pair of Air Jordans, all with tie samples wrapped inside. Plans on dispersing them out to the kids of the neighborhood. – a Markel idea as he was doing the same thing in LA. His motto was if the hood loves you, you're on to something. My creative team was interested in expanding our line, so I was checking the temperature a bit, to see if it got any friction. I was more so interested in manifesting doing business with Michael Jordan one day. Pulling up to the projects, memories filled my mental. The children crowded my driver's vehicle, eyes wide like Christmas morning. I knew we had to be quick, in and out.

"Everyone loves Jordans right?" I asked, teacher-style as the kids nodded their heads, eyes filled with gleam. I mean, it's not a normal day when someone pulls up to the hood dropping off Air Jordans and ties. "Ight, no shoving. No pushing, chill. There's plenty but you won't get anything if you can't do these two things…." There was silence. "Repeat after me. I welcome financial, emotional, spiritual and physical stability into my life." The kids repeated after me. "Good. I welcome love, success, inner peace and clarity into my life. Say it!" The kids followed suit, tripping over some words but ultimately completing the task.

"Second thing. There are ties in these sneakers. Bow ties and regular ties. You must promise me you will wear it. Give it to your dad, uncle, brother. Wear it around the house, to school, chillen on the playground…"

"Can I rock it on my head?" One of the smaller, class-clown type of kids asked from a crowd of faces which made everyone laugh.

"You sure can. Wear that shit on your head. Your ankle. Your wrist. Just wear it. Repeat after me, Prince Apparel!!" I emphasized as they followed suit, yelling back *Prince Apparel*. "Ight. Carry on and be good to each other. Love one another. Stay behind if you don't know how to wear a tie. I'll teach you."

We finished distributing the kicks and ties and it felt good. Felt right. Then I drove towards the projects where I grew up, fulfilling the other part of the Yonkers trip. The LOX marinaded the speakers as I cruised the New York streets. Pulling up on my older brother, I felt nothing. He was sitting there, doing nothing. Same stoop I last seen him. Three feens hung close to him like a scene from The Corner. Like maggots. Guess he was king of the feens, my twin brother Bruce. Older than me by two minutes. I sat there in the car briefly, just peeping the scenery. Reminiscing a little. You see, my mom loved Bruce Lee and Prince, therefore naming her only twin sons after the legends. Growing up, Bruce was the popular athlete who had all the girls. All of em. He had the height and was damn near injury proof. Bruce was so cool, he had kids giving him cool clothes and kicks to rock when I was stuck in suits. Even had NBA scouts looking at him once upon of time. Then, he decided to try to fill our father's footsteps and began selling drugs and had his little run. Then he began doing drugs. Not long after that, the streets swallowed him alive. That's the story of my brother. That's the legacy of Bruce Roberson. Yes, our father was shot in front of us and yes that shit was traumatizing and life altering but in life, we all had choices. All of us. Sink or fuckin swim. Two minutes later I was in stride heading towards my brother. He was now alone as the other feens scattered away like roaches. Bruce was in a sedated haze. He squinted towards me and kept quiet. Then looked off into the blue sky. Blotchy holes covered his skin.

"Bruce." Silence. Last time I had talked to him, he was asking for money, his usual. I told him *nah*, my usual. The deal was, if he wasn't going to complete the many drug programs available for him, I wasn't giving him money and funding his heroin habit. He made his choice. "You still mad at me big bro?" More silence. I just stared at him, reminding myself not to judge. Only God can do that. I was disgusted though. He smelled like urine. Looked like shit. I didn't appreciate how he stressed our mom out.

"I don't want your money." Bruce uttered, dreary eyed.

"That's good." I sat beside him.

"Don't want your funky ass tie neither." My brother growled, staring at the ten abstract ties I had drooped over my shoulders.

"Well." I placed a tie around his neck anyway. "You're getting one. Mom is cancer free." Bruce remained expressionless, still focused on the clouds as I sat there with him for about three minutes. Three long minutes. Then I finally stood to my feet. "You reek of shit my nigga."

"Get in your fancy car and go! I'll wipe my funky ass with this tie. Better yet, I'll use it to hang it up! That'll make you happy. Get out of here!"

I just looked back at my fraternal twin. The guy I used to look up to as a kid. The one I used to know. I chose my next words carefully because I'd probably never see him again. "I'm not going to allow you to make me have survivor's remorse. I'm also aware that my success can make you uneasy, you being my twin brother. My existence is proof that your addiction is a choice. I get it."

"You still telling people you saw Pops get killed? Still telling yaself that? You sat there and pissed and shitted on yourself. You cried and cried until snot dripped down your face. How come you never tell that part of the story huh? Never see that in your interviews and speeches. You still lying to the world?"

Questions that made me shake my head. The night my dad was murdered, me and Bruce were there. Four men came in the house dressed in black and hit my father with the butt of the gun. We watched them tie my father up and pour gasoline on him. I remember screaming and crying while gunman number two kept his gun on my brother and I. Bruce stood still, just breathing. *Shut up Prince. Try to shut up.* I remember him whispering as he stood in front of me. *Don't set my father on fire.* My brother was so brave, I remember. Gunman number one said something to Bruce which I can't remember, because I covered my ears and Bruce pointed to the gun. Then one of the gunmen walked Bruce to the hallway and they talked for a few minutes. Maybe about five. Never knew what they were talking about. Bruce came back to stand in front of me. Anger filled his eyes as he was huffing and puffing all while my dad yelled, *fuck away from my sons you bitch ass muthafukkas*!!! They hit my dad again as blood splattered everywhere. I was still crying, my eyes shut tight again. Balled up in the corner at this point. Heard my father yell *I Love You Sons.* Then I heard a sharp *bang* and that was that. You'd think that type of thing would bring brothers closer right? Just because he was braver than me in that moment, it made his experience more terrifying than mine? Made his story more tragic? Bruce never fucked with me. Ever. His own twin! Used to tell people he wished he was an only child. Like he pegged me his arch nemesis out of the blue. No one knows you better than the person you shared a twin bed with for majority of your childhood and he knew I just wanted to be his friend. Looking out the window towards my twin brother who was now tying my tie around his arm, I queued my driver to pull off. Fuck Bruce! I kept it moving because there's never much use reasoning with a feen. He could've had it all. Still could. He just doesn't want shit. He's happy sitting on a stoop in a dirty alley amongst shit, rats and feens and I'll never make that my muthafukkin problem.

5

feel like making love

Ne PM LA time, four PM Aruba time, I was hopping off my private jet to attend Chuck's wedding. My assistant and Markell rode with. The others were there already as they'd partook in the bachelor party festivities two nights prior. I opted outta that fuck shit of course. It wasn't until my foot touched Aruban soil when it hit me. The accountant of Prince Apparel was really marrying some bitch he just met. *Could you believe this shit?* Being the businessman I was, I ensured the men in the wedding were all dripped in my threads. Guess you could say I was 15% there to celebrate this mockery, 85% here to ensure my business followed through. Who was I kidding, ten/ninety. Bruce's conversation still lingered a bit, I ain't gonna lie but fuck that bum. He couldn't even crack a smile about our momma beating cancer. Fuck him. Now if he ever decided to change his life around then I'd embrace him, open arms. No apology needed but until that magical, majestical day fell upon us - fuck Bruce.

We sat there: Lyle, his wife, Markell, Omar, Bianca and me, in the lavish venue. Quiet as church mice, watching the wedding party sift in. Chuck knew better than to ask us to be in the wedding. Particularly, me. Couldn't help to think, must've been some superb pussy to have my boy crashing out like this.

"This wedding shit feels too much like turning yaself in. Chuck a wild boy."

Lyle whispered my way. I wasn't dignifying that shit with a response, so I just looked at this nigga. Not only was Lyle twice married, one of his wives sat on the other side of him. I whipped out my phone, texted some hos and checked a few emails. Lyle broke the silence again.

"Which red head is Chuck marrying again?"

"Either the one from the party at Naomi Campbell's or the one from Prince's shindig last month or from that pool party that time." Omar straightened his tie.

"Nah I think it's the girl from BET with the red bob." My assistant Bianca added, as she continued to text her man.

"I thought it was the ho that burnt him. She had that red hair he be going crazy about. He obviously fucked her." My disapproval was evident as I never support bad business.

"Well, we will all see when she comes down the aisle." Markell added as we grew silent again. Three minutes about. I broke that shit this time.

"You know we're going to have to console this muthafukka when this all goes to shit in about six months." All the coy shit was corny. We were watching our friend marry a stranger.

"Six? Three months tops," Lyle added.

"I give it two years. Typical Hollywood shit. Chuck ain't a complete fool." Bianca placed her bet.

"Yall bogus. Three weeks. Annulment. Shit gonna end all types of fucked up and on top of that, he's going to blame *us* for not stopping him." Omar predicted as we put in our bets. "What you think Markell?"

"Ten bands. They last forever."

Bullshit, Lyle fake coughed.

The flower girls were strolling past us, and we all waved in an uncle and aunt-like fashion. Chuck cut no corners, expense-wise. None.

It was the reception and Chuck and his bride were deeply engulfed in each other. Moreso a slide than a bride but to each its own. Markell was at the bar as I was indulging in steak bites and asparagus. The wedding was comical, but the food was hittin. The live band was playing something funky while I was timing out my exit. Markell was on his way back to the table when I watched him spill all four drinks onto this woman's white pant suit. It all seemed to happen in slow motion too. Drinks in the air, Markell on the ground; straight fumble. Hopping up to help the woman as Markell apologized, cleaning up endless spilled liquid. Her white attire, now brown due to the cognac.

"You ight? I apologize for my friend."

"Fuck you and fuck your friend."

The curvy woman in the white jumpsuit darted past me, outfit drenched in VSOP. She was livid, cursing and carrying on. When she brushed past me, I noticed she smelled good as shit which made her automatically alluring. Distinct dimples inverted both of her cheeks. She was pissed but she was pretty, so I grabbed her arm to get her attention. To get a closeup too, I'll keep it G.

"I apologize for my friend, for real." Staring in her eyes, she began to calm down a bit. Standing about 5'2, six-inch heels graced her feet as she looked up at me with deep slanted eyes.

"You can let go of me now." She smirked sarcastically, yanking back her arm and storming towards the exit.

"Fuck her."

I heard a voice from behind me. It was Markell with fresh drinks in his hand. I took back one as I made my way towards the exit to spy on Miss White Pantsuit. She was outside, blotting out her outfit as best as she could. Then she pulled out a cigarette, fury and defeat drenched.

"You're too pretty to smoke that shit."

"Fuck off." She was clearly still on demon time. I just smiled at her mean ass.

"Come here." I instructed as she looked at me as if I had three heads. She put that fuckin cigarette out though.

"I'm not interested."

"Fine. Stay there." Slipping off my black and burgundy suit jacket, I draped it over her shoulders. "Put this on. It'll go cool with your shoes and clutch."

She hesitated momentarily and then stood up to try it out, checking herself out in someone's side mirror. Then she walked back inside the wedding reception. Didn't say a word. Rude as shit. I went back in a few minutes later, ready to call my pilot. *Before I Let Go,* the original version glazed the spot as I scanned the room. Miss White Pantsuit was now sporting merely my suit jacket and heals. Floral black lace tights graced her curvy thighs and pretty legs. She looked fly, flyer than the original look. Catching my eyes, she sashayed towards me with new energy. A pristine smile coated her face and her ass was crazy fat.

"Thank you for saving my outfit and my evening."

"You're welcome. You feel better now?"

"Yes. Just been a long day. My cousin Chuck is marrying this stranger without a prenup, I have a migraine, some business fell through and on top of all of that my outfit being ruined just threw me off. I'm not usually a total bitch."

"Understandable. Now I see why I got that stray bullet. You look beautiful."

"Thank you."

The curvy goddess was now off enjoying the party as I sat next to Markell, eyes glued on shawty. I enjoyed watching her work the room. Keeping my eye on my new friend, playing it cool of course, I chopped it up with my team enjoying the band and drinks. Aruba was feeling decent right now. I danced with a few women that night but shawty's dance was most noteworthy. She could cut a rug too. The party lights flickered off her body while *Superman* by Black Coffee massaged our eardrums followed up with *Turn Me On*. I watched her dance like a lion scoping his prey. A few songs later I mustarded up the courage to grab her at the right moment. I got her for one song, Rini's *Aphrodite*. Sensual shit. Sliding behind her, I initiated my dance. Swaying to the melodies, I enjoyed my moment as we made small talk.

"My cousin Chuck is one of the brand ambassadors for this suit jacket you're letting me sport tonight ya know." Unaware of who I was, she thought she was educating me and it was sexy.

"Prince Apparel?" Pretending to be unaware, I watched her shake her head proudly.

"Yup. The irony. I believe it's their unique lining that makes them stand out. Rare African and Indian material. Gotta support black business."

I dug her, immediately. Something about her. Extending my hand out, I finally decided to properly introduce myself. "I'm Prince."

She blushed hard which brought out her dimples more, finally extending her well-manicured hand to shake mine. "So I cursed out *Mr Black Business* at my cousin's wedding. How fuckin embarrassing. Wait, so I'm guessing the oh-so-eloquent man who ruined my outfit is part of the team too?" We both looked over towards Markell.

"Along with those two guys over there. The short one in the lavender suit and the tall guy in the burgundy." I pointed towards Lyle and Omar.

"Oh I get it. So the cognac on my Versace pantsuit was yall version of *shy brother*." Her mean ass had jokes.

"Nah, not at all." A slight grin coated my face.

"So whom do I send my dry-cleaning bill? Him? You? Prince Apparel as a conglomerate?" She smiled, still teasing assumingly.

"You a standup comic? Fuck ya lil outfit, I'll buy you two more. You'd look nice in the black one paired with some Amina Muaddi heels." I inched a little closer towards her as she stepped back a bit, sizing me up.

"Good eye. That's why I own it in black....and gold."

"Oh yeah?"

"Mmm hmm. Burgundy too." She adjusted her bezzled out Audermars Piquet, flexing a bit. *Damn she smelled good as hell.*

"Well why you ain't rock them tonight? You was in that white upstaging the bride and shit." I pulled her close to me, still dancing. Tracing her body with my fingertips, she shivered a bit before draping her arms around my neck like ribbon. She massaged my neck as we swayed. "What's your name?"

"Ashley."

Chopping it up with my new friend, I learned that she was Chuck's first cousin, a sports agent for the

NBA and shared the same birthday as my great grandmother. Ashley had a chic condo on the hills and was a mover and shaker like me. Baby version of me. We talked for about ten minutes about everything and nothing simultaneously. It was strange but fly. Felt like I knew her for a long time. Chuck caught our chemistry and gave me the wink that it was cool to pursue if I was interested. He said his cousin was a smart cookie and then he was back engulfed into his new bride. Watching the sunset with my crew with Ashley standing a few feet away with her family, I kept gazing from the sunset back to Ashley, back to the sunset. A few feet away from her, Chuck was holding his bride tight. Markell was on Facetime with his wife and Lyle had one of his wives with him, Stacia. My assistant Bianca was hugged up with her man, so he clearly flew in. Omar had something pretty with grey eyes on his lap. Love was all around. At least love-ish. I don't know, maybe Markell was right - Chuck and whatsherface may last forever. Maybe my momma was right too. Everybody needs love. Everybody. Wrapping up the reception with fireworks and shots was a nice touch. Chuck even had doves and flamingos. Markell was still on facetime with his wife and babies which made me smile. Then I looked back at Ashley who was staring at me. She smiled and looked away. She singlehandedly saved Aruba for me, and I couldn't wait to call her when I got back to LA. We both were busy as shit so getting up was hard, but she did make a slight impression. She was a networker and an entrepreneur. Embracing her singleness with massive ambition; she matched my energy. It was two weeks later, a Thursday night when I called her. We had tried twice before then, to link up but shit always came up. This particular night she picked up on the second ring.

"Hello."

"It's Prince. What's up?"

She was quiet. "Yea I know. It's not a good time."

"You straight?" She was quiet again and I opted not to interrupt her silence.

"I just got…. I just got stood up." She blurted out in disbelief.

"What you mean?" I didn't like hearing her disappointed and couldn't imagine anyone standing her fine ass up. She grew quiet again.

"I'm lightly dating this football player and he was supposed to attend the BET awards with me and…he just called and bailed. Talking about a girlfriend he never mentioned before. Then tried to get me to sell my tickets to him so *they* can go! I just cursed him the fuck out. I'm pissed off. I avoid shit like this."

I laughed. Loud too.

"Fuck you."

"Nah, fuck him. I'm going with you."

"You are?" She was astonished.

"Yup. The universe wants us to."

Ashley grew silent again, I guess processing the sudden change. Then she said *okay* and that was that. Two hours later, I was at the BET awards with Ashley. She was beautiful in a rust-colored long dress that hugged her curves perfectly. I was dressed in some fly shit from Prince Apparel of course. We were both clearly single, so I was peeping my atmosphere. Spotted a few women I'd encountered in the past. Some a lil more recent than others. Everyone kept their cool. Saweetie was there looking like a Grammy. Definitely someone I manifested fucking in due time. She smiled my way for a quick sec too. Ashley walked off to go chat with Laz Alonzo for a few minutes. Probably mackin too. A lot of athletes were amidst due to All Star Weekend. I even seen my bro Shaq in the spot. The night was dope and of course I made sure I rubbed shoulders with a few people I needed to as it's always business as usual. Ashley, working in the NBA said her hellos to all the athletes. She had a Karen Civil type of demeanor, minus the scandals and finer. She was the homie. A beautiful homie and she was adamant on not giving me pussy right away. I liked that. A challenge.

"Thank you for coming with me." She leaned in towards me midway through the night.

"That's what friends are for. Thanks for having me."

I smiled looking at her. I left with something chocolate that night and Ashley left with Laz Alonzo. Told you - the homie. My homegirl Ashley. I still was on her ass though.

***

My accompanying Ashley to the BET awards, ignited us to connect. Our first date was fascinating as it was initiated by a mysterious text message out of the blue – an address. No hello, no grand rising, just an address. I'm a multimillionaire so I knew what women wanted and most times it wasn't really me; it's what I've acquired. Ashley was independent though. She didn't need shit from anybody. Looking towards the cryptic text, I shrugged and said fuck it. Pulling up to the address which happened to be a small restaurant that looked over the water, I was impressed. Set the tone to the tune of boundaries and mystique. We talked about our childhood, sports, and a little bit about her views on love. We talked about religion and spirituality and it was cool. She loved God. Deeply. The next date was at her spot as she invited me over and cooked dinner. We sat in her kitchen and talked for hours as she was ill at reading in between lines, dissecting everything I said. She saw through me and didn't judge me. She had an eloquent way of saying things and she listened. Not just to respond but truly listened. She was the conservative type. No long excessive weave. No crazy makeup and nails. Laser focused on her career and there wasn't any fucking going down. She made it crystal clear and that was cool. I simply got my pussy elsewhere, but my energy was on Ashley. My true friend. The most intriguing thing about her was she was the polar opposite of my ex. Ashley was short, brown and curvy. She followed through on her goals and was a good influence on a nigga. Sole', the complete opposite give or take. Ashley's genuine energy wiped out unnecessary distractions. Guess it's the God in her. One day I asked her to create a vision board of what she truly wanted and baby girl said she already had one. We exchanged collages and really were able to delve deep into our truest desires. Even told my therapist Lisa Swanson about her and she seemed to approve. The most magic thing about Ashley though was that when I was with her, I didn't have the visions. Well, there was only one.

I was at her house chillen and it was happening again. The *panic attacks*. I walked off towards the bathroom to splash water on my face as I counted down from fifty. Sole's whispers rippled through my brain in waves but I tuned her out. *You love me. You fuckin love me. It's spewing from your pores. Just look at you.* I tuned the voices out giving myself time but not too much time as I wasn't home. I was on a date with the perfect woman. Eventually I headed out the bathroom where Ashley was standing there in the doorway. Her cat circled by her feet.

"You okay?"

"Yeah, I'm good." I shifted my weight from leg to leg, nervously.

"Here." She leaned in to kiss my lips and all of a sudden, my heart stabilized. "Better?"

I just looked at her as my nerves relaxed. A swoosh of sedation coated my nerves and I felt safe. This woman was a goddess. Better yet an answered prayer. My best fuckin friend. She made tacos as we sipped wine. Keeping it innocent, I rubbed her pretty feet and we fell asleep to Boomerang that night. Her passionfruit candles massaging my senses. Waking up to her Doberman Pinscher and Siamese cat staring me down, I quietly grabbed my stuff and kissed Ashley on the forehead. Then I went back home. I'll keep it G and confess I got some pussy from a Jane Doe once I got back to the crib, nonetheless that was my last hallucination since the universe introduced me to queen Ashley.

Date two / three was fight night and she picked me up from my office. Hopping in her whip we rode out and about fifteen minutes in, I casually slid her a gift box. Lauryn Hill marinated her speakers.

"What's this?" She glanced down at the rectangular box at a red light.

"Yours."

"Not only is he fine but he bares gifts?!" She smiled unravelling ribbon, displaying the diamond bracelet. Her eyes lit up as she gave me a long, sensual kiss. Kiss number two baby. "Thank you. I love it Prince. Very playa."

I dripped the bracelet around her wrist, alongside her other diamonds as her smile was priceless. She couldn't stop grinning as we walked in dripped in furs and diamonds, all black everything. She had on a black leather catsuit. I was blacked out on my Shaft shit. Even spotted Omar there in a grey fur, something Nubian-like on his arm. We took our seats and sorta like the BET awards, dispersed doing our own thing. Both being master networkers, understood each other's careers. Walking back towards our seats, Ashley was seated, legs crossed. Her caramel thighs resembled honey buns from the bodega and I immediately grew hungry. She resembled a thick Nia Long, so fuckin pretty. I kept it cool though. I had some money on the fight, so I was in a zone as I noticed Ashley was quiet the entire time. I watched her pretty ass focus on the fight with extreme intensity. I was even deeply engulfed in her when Jervonte knocked his opponent out in the fourth round. Won me eighty bands. Easy. Ashley hopped up with the quickness, cheering and screaming as the fight wrapped up. It wasn't until the car ride home when she revealed she had won fifteen grand on betting on the fight. She had me mentally and physically stimulated at this point.

Baby girl was a gambler like me! What made it worse was when she reiterated that she won one hundred-fifteen grand, not fifteen. Oh, she was big dawg.

"You gotta come to the tables with me pretty."

"Aww, that's so sweet but I got this. I love my bracelet though." She smiled sweetly.

Sheesh. Rubbing my goatee, I looked towards her. "Cool ass Ash."

She blew me a kiss and turned on some Earth Wind and Fire for the ride. Did I mention she drove a bumblebee yellow and black SRT?. Oh ight. She was all the way legit. Probably why one Thursday we were going for a walk and she asked me to attend a cookout with her. It wasn't really my tempo but shit, fuck it.

"You gonna wear a suit or will I be able to see you in regular clothes?"

"I love my suits." I smiled her way.

"Oh I love them too. I just want to see you switch it up. You don't have to be Superman all the time. Be Clark Kent for a while."

I understood what she meant. She wanted to see the other side of a nigga but moreso she didn't want everybody to know who I was, so the day of her cookout

I tossed on an Amiri sweatsuit, white tee and some Jordans, a New York Knicks fitted on my head. Shit I'd play ball in. Athleisure but I iced it out a bit. Pulled up with a few cases of Henny black as she greeted me sporting a long-sleeved black maxi dress. Chuck and his bride Angela were there as well as her father. Cool guy. We played dominos, backgammon, drank brown and ate ribs and it wasn't so bad. Had she swindled me into a *meet the parents'* event without letting me hit, perhaps vetting me out too? Maybe, I had a nice time nonetheless. I went home and slipped back into a suit of course. Business as fuckin usual.

6

the line

It was a Wednesday and I decided to test Ashley a little. I just needed to truly see if I was putting twenty on ten when it came down to this woman. I was knocking down a few Jane Does but Ashley always lingered a bit. Not in a toxic way but differently. Our chemistry was dope and though we started off intense, her energy was light and easy. She was my sweetheart and as sexy as she was on fight night, had me feeling her even more.

I invited Ashley to come play spades with me at Markell's mansion on some double date shit. Me Ashley Markell and his wife. If she could pass this test, man listen sky's the limit. Walking through the palm tree filled courtyard towards the entryway, past an outdoor fire feature constructed out of a 12,000-pound boulder granite fire rock with binoculars. A few feet away, the "invisible" garage, we eventually made our way towards Markell's rotunda den – a separate feature from his mansion. Ashley followed close behind me, then she stopped me in my tracks.

"We are special friends, right?" She looked up at me with the face of an angel. I could tell she needed a little clarity and didn't want to sound corny about it. Maybe she was a bit nervous. She wanted the title for sure.

"We are." I pulled her close kissing her lips, then her neck.

"Cool. Don't be mad when I whoop your ass tonight in these here cards." Changing her tone, she led the way into Markell's crib, darting towards Donnie.

"Wait. You're my partner...."

Ashley was in the wind now giving Donyale a big hug, orchestrating the game and claiming her partner. I thought it was fly how she did it too. Markell greeted me with a smile, peeping it all as I admired Ashley's alpha female energy, respecting the play. Markell was my partner for the night. Girls versus guys. Not the plan, but now it was. Ashley's way. Donyale was dark skin with long locks and beautiful features, Markell's rock and she and Ashley hit it off right away and were acting like sisters. Ashley was fond of Donnie's afterhours lounge and was excited to place a face to the evolving establishment. She loved the crab balls. We kicked back in the den which was completely at odds with every other well-considered room in the house – a house that operated a strict no-shoe policy. The ladies trashed Markell and I in spades that night but we whooped they asses in three games of pool. Donyale glazed into her husband's lap as Ashley and I just enjoyed ourselves. Chopped it up about Markell and Donyale's Jerusalem wedding a few years back. Basking in good times. Discussed music and art. Chatted about Markell spilling the drinks on Ashley at Chuck's wedding. Had a good laugh about that as Ashley just smiled, acting like she didn't curse us out in Aruba.

"You two are so blessed to have one another." She sparkled a bit. This was it. The cure. Thank you God for Ashley.

"This is going to be yall in a few years." Donyale predicted, interrupting my thoughts.

"What you mean Donnie?" I asked my sis-in-law, attempting to hide my smile.

"Married with kids. You know the shit. Black love." Donyale grinned kissing Markel on the cheek.

"Prince has about five more years of pimpin left in him. I don't know girl." Ashley winked as we laughed a bit. She fit in like a glove. Classy and sexy.

"That isn't true." I looked towards this queen.

"Oh yeah?"

Maxwell's *Ascension* marinaded the room in perfect timing as Ashley glazed her head on my shoulder. Donnie was hosting, passing out devilled-eggs and Markell was on the sax, doing his jazz thing, sounding like shit, between jokes and politics. The night was love. Smooth. Only way to describe it.

"This Prince's favorite singer right here." Markell played *Left and Right* by D'Angelo, Redman and Method Man all while one of Markell and Donnie's twins tiptoed into the room.

"Uncle Prince!!!" She yelled jumping in my lap.

"Siya!! What you doing up Princess?" I embraced my goddaughter. The purest feeling.

"Siya Vanessa Livingston, why are you up at this hour? Get back in that bed unless you want to help me put these feathers on these hooks."

Donnie was kneeling in front of a giant board of endless feathers as she was in the beginning stage of creating her own earring line. Siya jumped up and down, excited to help as her twin sister Samia came out a few moments after. She gave me a sleepy hug and even gave Ashley one too. Then melted into her dad's lap with a yawn. I slipped them both some money while all the women in the home, minus Samia who was now falling asleep in her dad's arms, began creating earrings. Ashley was enjoying herself, engaging with Siya and Donnie. What a vibe.

The next weekend we went out on Markell's speedboat and just chilled. Ashley kicked back with me as Markell and Donnie sat up front, all parties enjoying the wind. Markell kicked up speed as Ashley held me tight, her arms around my waist. Donnie was enjoying the wind in her long locs with her husband. I embraced Ashley who wouldn't admit it but seemed a little scared on the boat. Pulling her close to me, reassuring her that I got her, she calmed down a bit and enjoyed the ride. Every night with her was a hit and I ain't even hit!

Now the night of the Prince Apparel fashion show was an interesting night. I pulled up with Ashley on my arm. Peeped Lyle and Chuck on the red carpet near the step and repeat, everyone looked clean. The line was crazy which was always a great thing. Everything was everything. Tonight was going to be the shit. Grabbing for Ashley's hand, I led the way. We didn't even make it ten feet when three men dressed in all black barged their way towards the crowd. Guns in their hands, I was triggered but I was with Ashley so fuck my feelings. *Bang bang bang bang*! Why the fuck was this happening on the night of my fashion show? Fuckin haters. The crowd scurried as the once line that dripped around the block to see my show had dissolved. Everyone was running for their lives. Ashley clutched my hand as we hauled ass back towards the car. Disarray all-around. No one was hurt, just a few shots in the air but the night was a bust and the venue was shut down. Ashley panting in my arms was priceless though. I held her tight while I signaled my driver to pull off. I'd deal with the paperwork of this bullshit another fuckin night. Quick reschedule and venue switch. Nothing too deep.

The following weekend was Karl Kani's rooftop birthday party and nothing beats a Karl Kani party. Nothing. His parties always contained beautiful, successful people who operated on a certain frequency.

Everyone was dripped down as tonight I chose to sport a teal and black floral-styled tuxedo – very clean. Karl's parties were always dope so I was looking forward to celebrating another black successful king and kickin it with my peers and mentors. I lived for this shit. My sweetie Ashley on my arm, the scent of cotton candy sifted from her skin and a canary and black tiger-striped dress hugged her body. Distinctive material sleeveless turtleneck-style which stopped midthigh. A slither of side boob, strappy ribbon stilettos that caressed her calves, she was dressed to kill. Nothing she could ever wear could hide them curves. Breathtaking as usual. Once in the elevator car I pushed the *close door* button, ensuring no one followed us. Sometimes you need the elevator to the face. Heading up seventeen stories towards the sky to the rooftop event, we kissed as I massaged her soft ass. That pussy was warming up just for me.

"Thank you for inviting me." She smiled coming up for air.

"No brainer." I winked and once we arrived, she squeezed my hand.

"Just like the BET awards and fight night?" She looked me in my eyes, referring to our network event demeanors – business first, then collab.

"Except you're coming home with me this time."

I squeezed her hand back and we went our separate ways, working the room. She wasn't my lady but the way things were looking., she'd soon be. Tonight, I felt like was the night she would finally let me tap that chocolate ass and if that shit hittin, then we really on to something. I'd been wining and dining the hell out of her and having a ball doing so. It's fun splurging on a woman who has her own. Shit, my pleasure. I watched her fine ass serenade the room as Eric Sermon's *Just Like Music* massaged our ears until I was interrupted by Lyle who, not even twenty minutes into the party had just locked a business deal with fraternity Omega Psi Phi, catapulting our company to new heights. My nigga Lyle. Never shocked when it came to my boy. Always a clean swish with my youngin. Always pure excellence.

"My niiiig. My noble intelligent G! Very fuckin nice."

I dapped him up and gave my boy his well-earned flowers as we mingled a bit and dispersed. The room, colorful and alluring as Mos Def's *Ms Fat Booty* danced through the airwaves and kissed our eardrums. Mini crabcake sandwiches danced on bronze plates alongside all types of sushi. A fruit buffet nearby. Naked women smeared in red, black and green paint decorated like the Tribe Called Quest *Low End Theory* album cover, slithered throughout the spot like floating art. Coming to America was muted on a jumbo theatre screen in the cut. Queen Latifah was on the mic hosting.

Rosie Perez floated through with Angie Martinez walking towards the alfredo dining area. Nas came in with AZ which was very dope to see. Idris Elba and his wife were there. Fashion goddess June Ambrose too. Channing Tatum, Mark Wahlberg and Jessica Alba was in the building. Teyana Taylor and Karrueche were at the bar sifting hookah. I even spotted Kevin Gates in the cut rolling trees. Karl always knew how to put it together just right. Sanaa Lathan's fine ass walked by as I saw her heading towards Omar and I spotted the play. *Very nice my boy, very nice.* My phone buzzed when I happened to be building with Spike Lee and it was Maria via text. *I'm terminating the pregnancy.* News to a nigga's ears! I sent her ten bands for doing the right thing. Another five racks to appreciate the fact that she was now blocked and continued on. She could keep her job as she cleaned the yacht good, I guess. Now I could forget this bitch existed and my *walk past you like I ain't fuck the dogshit outta you* game was immaculate. Karl Kani made his entrance a few moments later as we gave him the applause he deserved. Lights, cameras, action. The party kicked up a notch. Even the lighting changed for dramatic effect. Markel, Karl and I chopped it up for a moment over by the saltwater rooftop pool and then dispersed, enjoying the night. Diddy floated in about thirty minutes after that followed by my true mentor Andre Leon Talley. The goat. Cherry on the cake were the fireworks spelling out Karl Kani in the sky. Pretty fly especially with the four Hennessey fountains swirling and Tupac's *California Love* bumpin through the speakers. Clearly party of the year and it was only eleven o clock.

I was heading towards the bathroom when I ran directly into them. The last two people I'd ever thought I'd see in the universe. It was Sole' locked hands with a tall Asian man. Suit by Z Zenga. Armani tie. My ex dripped in a simple burgundy plunge dress that stopped at her knees. Hair parted up the middle, bone straight. Diamonds dripped her wrist and ears. Eloquent. The Sole' I knew was edgy so I didn't know who the fuck this librarian was standing before me. Was this real? Was this another fuckin vision? It had to be real because I hadn't had visions since I'd been with Ashley. Shit, a nigga been getting better sleep too.

"Prince Roberson of Prince Apparel. I'm a big fan."

My ex's man extended his hand to me exuding genuine energy. Shaking his hand, I looked towards my ex, confusion coating my face. I couldn't read her expression. I ain't know her anymore. Standing tall at 5'10, model-esque. Dark lips, a jewel on her forehead. Sultry vibes. Like the late *Aaliyah*. Sole' was standing in front of me. The actual her. Her man's lips were moving but I couldn't' hear a word. Like some paradox universe. Standing there in front of my ex and her man felt like a nightmare. He clearly knew nothing of me and was networking. Sizing my ex up discreetly, a diamond on her finger. A smile on her lips as she squinted as if she didn't know me at all. I'll keep it real and admit I was hurt. I don't know why. A sharp sting shot throughout my body, like lightning. My ex-love leaned in towards her lover as I shifted my weight from leg to leg, uneasily. *What the fuck Prince!* My confidence gushed towards the floor – invisible liquid on our feet. Exposed. Naked. Felt like a little boy. I began to sweat, as my ex's beau was still talking yet I couldn't hear him. His lips were indeed moving. Where the fuck was my team with the alleyoop? Shit, anybody. Get both these muthafukkas away from me. All I could do was internally plead.

"You okay man?"

"Yeah, you okay?"

Sole' followed up clutching her man's hand. Defeat. Pure defeat drenched from my pores but then the tempo shifted. It happened all of a sudden. I felt a swoosh of wind as there was new energy and no longer a party of three. No longer a third wheel scenario. I was no longer the odd man out. There was my alleyoop and thank God she wore that dress. Here was Ashley. I came with her, but her reappearance did something to the moment. Maybe it was the yellow dress. Maybe it was just her.

"Hey you!" She hugged me sweetly and reached her hand out towards Sole' and her dude. "I'm Ashley.

How are you beautiful people?" Pure goddess energy spewed from this woman.

"I'm Mike, this is Sole'."

"Did I hear a Thai accent?"

"Good ear, that's where I'm from." Mike gleamed professionally before they both began to have a complete conversation in Thai. Whatever Ashley was saying had Mike grinning, laughing and glowing. Standing next to him, a perspiring Sole'. She wasn't the star of this show and since I'd known her, she never liked that shit.

"I..I..I love your dress," Sole' stuttered attempting to add her two cents, searching for relevancy.

"Oh, thank you." Ashley grinned glazing over Sole's tall physique. "I like…. your perfume. Prince, I've gotta make a few contacts. We'll link later babe." Kissing my cheek sweetly, she said goodbye to Sole' and Mike. In and out. A ray of fuckin light. Changed the energy all the way up and it was exhilarating seeing Sole' stand next to a woman iller than her. I dispersed away to chop it up with Omar and Markel and enjoy Karl's party with new energy. Baffled by tonight's events but more so intrigued by Ashley's effortless power. She was chopping it up with Lala as I watched her from afar. She was the golden ticket and I had to wife her. The right way. I found myself near the bathroom still trippin off Ashley when I ran right into Sole' except she was alone this time. I blocked the entrance to the bathroom, playfully.

"Move out my way before I pee on your feet." She brushed past me into the bathroom. Now *that* was the Sole' I knew. I went to go drain the main vein and we came out the restrooms concurrently. We catch eyes, she rolls hers and keeps it moving.

"Ex-girlfriend how ya been?"

"Prince." Sole' peeked back with a meek smile.

"Reach out if you need anything and thank you for sending my mother the Christmas cards." I extended my card to her. Sadness was in her eyes. Maybe despair from Ashley chopping her pretty little head off a few minutes prior. Shit, she's a pothead so maybe it was simply good drugs but there was something in her eyes. She grabbed my card and looked over it as I traced her wrists.

"I'm good." She handed it back to me, stepping backwards towards the wall.

"You sure?" I walked up close on her, Hennessy black swirling through a nigga. As much as this bitch had been plaguing and haunting my mind, fuck it. Will Smith's *Summertime* had the spot jumpin and all you see is big booties, sweat, and everyone having the best time.

Her breathing began to intensify as she melted into the wall, her eyes locked on mine.

"Oh I'm real good. You're not though."

Sole' pointed towards Ashley who was watching me sweat my ex from across the party. Sole' slipped away smoothly and dispersed into the crowd as Ashley looked confused with a hint of agitation. Busted. I was single but I was busted. Felt busted. Ashley made her way towards me as I grew nervous. I played that shit cool though and so did she.

"You enjoying yaself?" She smiled, embracing me.

"Now I am."

"I need to chat with you later." She smiled dancing with me a bit. Then I was pulled away by a business associate, yet my mind was going. What did she have to talk to me about? Was she cutting me off? Nah, her fine ass wasn't cutting me off. What type of time was she really on though? Of course, when I was done chatting, she was now tied up networking. Four songs later I found myself looking off into the night stratosphere by the pool taking back a shot. Omar was puffing a cigar nearby, enjoying the quiet time too. Then I heard a voice.

"Hey you." It was Ashley.

"What you need to talk to me about?" I got straight to the point as Omar walked away towards the party.

"Look at me." She demanded as I turned around and looked at her. "You love that girl. The model girl in the burgundy dress." Ashley looked me straight in the eyes.

"You asking or telling?"

"See now you're playing with me." She was serious, so serious. Face of an angel and pretty as shit under the glimmery pool lights and ripples of the water.

"Untrue."

"Swear?"

"I'm tunnel vision, laser focused on you. I swear on my life."

"Fuck that. Swear on *my* life."

"Blow style baby?" I smiled referring to her favorite Johnny Depp film. Walking up close on her. She melted in my arms, enjoying our embrace while I kissed her lips. Then I put my lips towards her ear.

"*Shhhh*. My secret is I don't want you with anyone else either. I ain't gonna hurt your heart. I'd be a fool to hurt your heart." I guess the Hennessy was floating through her too because two minutes later Ashley was leading me to the corner bathroom in the cut, hiking her dress up.

"I can't wait any more. This good girl shit is killing me. Lock that door and gimme that dick." Ashley turned around kissing me as I massaged her body. Then I turned her back around and gave her what she needed and what I needed. Shit what the world needed. Ass was crazy fat and I bust her down, one leg up. Pussy was the bomb too! A good fuck and her corporate ass needed it. Someone was knocking which interrupted our session, or at least tried to. We kept going. Stumbling out the bathroom after our quickie, I went first and then she followed me and in true sickomode fashion, Sole' and Mike were there because apparently he had to take a shit and the main bathroom was full. Mike slipped in modestly as jealousy coated Sole's face and Ashley was grinning ear to ear, body probably pulsating feeling amazing. Sole' remembers the ride. Glowing and shit.

"Goodnight Sole'. Prince babe let's get outta here." Ashley whined sexily as we brushed past everyone who didn't matter. Ashley was the don and had successfully slayed the dragon that is Sole'. Someone stuffed the birthday cake in Karl's face and got stomped all the way out for it, Lyle made Prince Apparel some bread, Omar got Sanaa's number and Markell lost his twenty-thousand-dollar diamond ring. What a fuckin night. Happy Birthday Karl Kani. Did I mention I love Karl's parties?

Ashley got a work call so we couldn't have sex again immediately but she attended the rescheduled version of the Prince Apparel fashion show with me and it was a beautiful night, parallel to my beautiful life. Shit, one day maybe she'd be my beautiful wife.

7

one mo gin

Two nights later, Omar stopped by to kickback and build. We debated about sports and played a game of pool. Grabbed some drinks and then went to my movie theater, tossed on his movie of choice and chilled.

"Prince."

"What's on ya mind Omar?"

He was silent until he wasn't. "I can't have kids."

"Okay." My response as there's nothing to really say about something like that.

"I can't have kids and I'm really feelin Sanaa and I … I don't know."

My boy was obviously having an internal struggle and I was amateur on the topic so I chose not to throw around shallow advice. Looking up at the screen, the movie Blade serenaded the theater as fine ass Sanaa Lathan stepped on the scene. Omar's eyes were glued, clearly infatuated. I couldn't correlate how him not being able to have kids had anything to do with him and Sanaa but just because I was ignorant to it didn't mean it wasn't valid. Shit, to my knowledge him and Sanaa had just met.

"Adopt. There are a million kids out here with no homes. A rich, black, cool dad? Shit, sounds like a foster kid's dream."

My suggestion was cut short as Omar's phone began to ring. Sanaa's name popped up on the screen causing him to light up like a jack-o'-lantern. He took the call into the hallway while I observed his energy shift. The conversation must've been going great because he was grinning, laughing, not a concern in the world. My boy was dating an actress and it looked like it was serious. Guess cupid was shooting everyone in the ass. Love, ha.

***

The next day I was at my headquarters handling business. The Knicks were playing on a nearby plasma, which I had bets on so I had my good eye on that. Everything else was business as usual.

"Prince. You have a visitor."

My assistant Bianca poked her head in my office and tiptoed away. I had one meeting in two hours, so I was unsure of who was visiting me. Maybe it was Ashley on her spontaneous shit again. If so, I was laying dat ass out right on my desk, word up. I smiled at the thought of her putting that pussy on me in the bathroom at Karl Kani's birthday party. Had plans to do it the right way later on tonight. She ain't seen shit yet. Would I wife her? As cool as she was during spades night and on the speed boat, sexy as she looked on my arm at the fight, pretty as she looked at the fashion show and how smoothly she handled Karl's party? Colossal chance. That pussy was good too. Deeper than that, she was soul food and I wasn't fucking this one up. She was stiff competition. Ashley was ill. I could even picture my mom liking her. She even had Sole' stuttering and shit. Fuck was she doing there anyway? I know one thing; Ashley and that leopard dress stole the night. My baby Ashley. None of these hos had shit on her. Envisioned myself taking her back to Aruba where we met and making it official there. That would be fly. Parasail with her, swim with the dolphins, ATVs, sightsee, ziplining, whatever she wanted. I reminded myself to have Bianca send Ashley some white roses to her job. Then I checked my watch, recollecting plans to go shoot hoops with the fellas around three as I walked out to meet my uninvited guest. I stopped abruptly in my tracks.

"Hey." Hair twisted up in two buns. Red matte lips. Distressed jeans and a Tupac t-shirt cut up into a crop top. Tiny face gems traced her face like tribal art. It was her. It was Sole' again. I blinked a few times to ensure I wasn't seeing things.

"Fuck you doing here?" My initial reaction.

"That's rude." Chanel lingered from my old lover.

"Where's your man?"

"Not here. Where's your girl?"

"I'm single."

"You didn't look single."

"She's a special friend." I watched my ex mind my business in disbelief. She had a whole boyfriend. Fuck was wrong with this crazy girl?! Me and Ashley would laugh about this shit later while I eat sushi off her body.

"Special. Hmm...Well, she's pretty." Sole' brushed past me towards my office. Tracing her fingertips across my oak desk, gazing off into my built-in aquarium.

"Yeah ya dude seemed impressed." I just watched her. Twenty seconds later, she spun around to face me.

"Am I interrupting anything?"

My life bitch, my truest feeling yet out my mouth spewed, *I was about to eat some lunch.*

"Ooo you know what I want?"

"You've never known what you've wanted a day in your life and you expect me to have that information?"

Sole' just rolled her eyes. "Shut up. I want Sonic." A big smile coated her face.

Back in college we used to stuff our faces with Sonic while we studied. Her major was law at that time, mine business management and communication. Sole' was my beautiful brainiac. The shit that would take me hours to do, she'd complete in 45 minutes. She'd do little weird, sexy shit like want to fuck really bad but I had homework, so she'd just do my homework for me and then we'd be back to fucking. She quit school sophomore year after changing her major a million times but lived in my dorm with Markell and I for about a year until I saved up to get my own place. Markel was usually at his college shawty's dorm so it worked out. They nicknamed us *The Fugees* on campus because we rolled three deep back then on the Prince Apparel tip. I was the only one out of the three who graduated. Me and Sole' were inseparable - back in college that is. My wild girl. Flower child. I looked at the stuffed shells Ashley had packed me for lunch as they were becoming obsolete by the second. Ashley was still my sweetheart, I just had to wrap some shit up with my old work real quick. I'd see her pretty ass tonight. Sole' ordered us some Sonic as we reminisced.

"Truth or dare?" Sole' bit into her chili dog making a mess, sauce all over the place. I grabbed a nearby wipe and with one single swipe my desk was clean again.

"Grow up."

"Loosen up. Truth or dare?" She reiterated not missing a beat.

"Why?"

"C'mon."

"What's your angle? You come in here with your bullshit and ya baby hairs and mini mouse buns and chili dogs and your fuckin kiddie games." She just stared at me with them eyes. Those familiar fuckin eyes. "Dare." I gave in loosening my tie, ready for whatever. Suck her toes, take her down right here on my desk. Whatever she wanted me to do I was wit it so she had better make it good.

"I dare you to fire that girl from the party."

I looked deep in her eyes. My jealous lil Sole'. Some things never change. Had the nevre to follow it with a *I mean, only if you don't love her of course.* She sat back in her seat watching me dial up Ashley. If it was going to get me that pussy which I had a feeling it might, fuck it. Last time I felt this way, I won a quarter million at an underground poker game in Harlem. Last time I felt this way, I won my yacht. Yeah she was slingshotting me the pussy pretty much. She's a narcissist so she just needed a little leverage or at least the illusion of leverage. Life decisions in real time. Sole' was staring at me; disbelief coated her face. She didn't think I could do it. She thought I was bluffing. She ain't know I was that nigga for real. Ashley picked up quickly with a simple *hey babe*.

"What's up. Look, I need a little bit of space. You're beautiful and perfect and I'm not trying to hurt you, but I need space. Work shit. A lot of work shit. Space and time. Ok? Ight cool." I hung up cold as ice as Sole' looked a bit taken back. Impressed even. If I didn't know her as well I'd say my doing that made her pussy wet. "Only because I'm not *in* love with her. Truth or dare?" It was my turn to ask.

"I said fire her not put her on ice but I'll let you have that. Truth."

"You miss me?"

"Yes. Weak question. Truth or dare?"

"Fine. Better question. You threatened by Ashley?" I looked her in the eyes.

"Was that her name?"

"Yeah."

"Not anymore. Truth or dare Prince."

"I don't wanna play this shit anymore."

"I know you don't. Truth or dare."

"Dare."

"Kiss me."

"Hell no." A devilish grin coated my face. "I wanna kiss them other lips."

"I know you do. I want you to kiss me though," Sole' purred.

"I'm not wit ya fuckin games Sole'. This ain't college. Look around, we're grown." I poured myself some scotch.

"I kiss him to get him to stop talking. If he keeps talking, I will love him and I don't want to love him. I really don't. As strategies go, it's not my finest. Kissing is just another way of talking except without the words." Sole' quoted Nicole Yoon, taking my drink back.

"Good read."

"Yeah I know, I put you on. Kiss me Prince."

"Nah, I recall putting you onto that one."

"Yeah whatever."

She whispered crawling onto the desk, feline-like, eventually kissing my mouth. Ethereal energy breathed through me as the world made sense instantly. I wrapped my arms around her slender body, pulling her closer to me and kissed her deep. Pouring her body into mine. My baby was back. My real baby, if only for a little while and if I was dreaming. Fuck it. The kiss was euphoric, I slipped her my address as she told me I owed her a real date. After that she was in the wind. My Sole'. The prettiest plot twist with ten toes. Life was marvelous.

***

Later that night was my date with Sole' and I had my chef cook a lavish meal. It was actually the spread I had set up for Ashley, but plans had changed and if you don't know why I chose Sole', then you just don't get it. I had to keep it real with myself, I wasn't getting anywhere with Ashley or anyone for that matter until I acknowledged my unfinished business with my ex-girlfriend. Part of me just wanted to hit the pussy one more time, I ain't even gonna hold you. Nostalgia pussy be the best. I had sushi and lobster and plenty of veggie rolls. In the final hour I decided to whip something up myself. I mean, it was Sole'. You pull out all the stops for Sole'. I just hoped she wouldn't stand me up. My mind was swirling as I needed to get everything just right. Perfect. Her favorite fruit was mango so I had plenty of that. Favorite color was yellow so I had the florist kick up on the gold and mustard decor. Her favorite film was Love Jones, a story about black love. A movie about two starving artists. Hmm… what would Darrius Lovehall do? Play it easy, nonchalant-almost. Putting on some smooth jazz as I reflected on my ex's favorite love story film, attempting to replicate the vibe, I couldn't believe myself. I was behaving like a teenager. Couldn't believe I still had a crush on this girl. Fifteen minutes past eight, my doorbell was ringing as her mystical ass was on time. She glossed in, a mauve colored Grecian goddess skirt wrapped her body, one thigh exposed. Same color material wrapped her breasts and neck, bandage-like. Waist beads of seashells draped her belly and thigh. Two buns in her hair except loose water ringlets floated down her face this time. She was here. Three minutes later after an awkward *church hug*, I was giving her a tour of my home. Walking past the spiral staircase and elaborate chandelier, we started at the wet bar to unwind. Dusse' was her choice. Stop two, my study to chill and talk. Both built-in fireplaces lit because I always enjoyed watching her skin glisten under candlelight. We spent a lot of time in the library in college, so this felt evocative. We sipped on brown like back in the day and kicked back under the mahogany shelves. Shoes off. One leg kicked up on a nearby bean sofa. Her toes melted into the plush carpet as she sifted through endless books.

"Your *beautiful distraction*. Isn't that what you used to call me back in college?" Liquor swirled through the both of us as she reminisced.

"You used to suck my dick and do my homework for me. Could you ever truly be a distraction?"

"I spoiled you, I'll own that. Me doing your work for you wasn't conducive but back to my original point, that's what you had me saved as in your phone and for the muthafukkin record, you always were weak at asking for sex so that was my way of helping you get it going." She popped her shit as no one popped shit quite like Sole'. "Plus, back then you were my sexy geek protégé that was rough around the edges but still super refined. It's those Libra and Taurus placements in your chart."

"Don't know what that means." I laughed at her depiction of me and astro mumbo jumbo.

"Means I used to enjoy being your cheerleader. I loved rooting for you."

She was on the floor engulfed in my rug, feelin the drink she was babysitting. She could never hold her liquor, the reason she smokes. Her eyes engulfed in a book. Her long legs in the air, toes pointed. Twin towers. I reminisced about those legs. A million sexy stories bout those legs.

"Goddess Girl…. Oshun… Asshole… Yoruba… Her… Soul Snatcher… Big Baby… My Wife. Let's just say I had you saved under a variety of things over the years until you changed your number."

"You know the difference between you and me?"

"I follow through on what I say and you, not so much?" She ain't find that one funny.

"Nah, I would've read all these books as opposed to using it for decoration for when my *smart* friends stopped by." She giggled at her own joke as I watched her read. Her eyebrows would go up every time she stumbled across an interesting detail. It was when I caught her staring at me when she hopped up. Guess she'd grown restless. "I'm hungry."

"That's good. I cooked."

Sole' knew I could get busy in the kitchen, so she wasn't fazed. She knew ya boy had skills. Walking past my bathroom, a room with a copper tub surrounded by classic Brazilian tiles and other local flourishes as well as a his and hers sink which was near a room filled with an ad hoc arrangement of film posters and bistro tables; we finally hit the kitchen. Sleek and regal with a unified color scheme. I kept it simple with a honey garlic marinade drizzled over salmon with Italian seasoned asparagus. Parmesan sprinkled on top. Italian noodles too alongside a lobster salad. Sole' climbed on my marble kitchen island, gracefully spreading her body out doing yoga poses. She hated rules.

"What you doing up there?" I inquired doing my chef shit.

"This is *tree pose*. This is *cobra*. This is *bridge*. This is *warrior*." She displayed different stretches." I wanted her in the *downward doggy,* but it wasn't time for all that.

"It's funny. This is how I envisioned life with you. This picture right here."

I created a square with my hands as if I was capturing a polaroid of this beautiful creature filled with so much history. Couldn't stop reminiscing on our love story. She ate and stretched as we discussed funny college moments for a bit.

"You, Markell and Troy had them stupid high-top fades. Eraser-head ass crew." Sole' hiked a lil.

"We were the shit too, don't leave that part out and we won't even get into you, Rachel and Brenda attempting to bring bell bottoms back. Epic fail." I tossed a piece of lobster at her as she failed to catch it in her mouth.

"Remember my white thigh high leather boots? You used to love me in them damn boots." She smiled my way. I just looked at her fine ass admiring her nostalgic power. She knew I remembered them boots. She rode my dick a couple times in them boots.

"Remember our picnics on the bleachers?"

"I remember everything about us."

After dinner we strolled towards my movie theatre and watched an old black and white film of her choice, Casablanca. Wasn't my thing, but she loved that shit and I always loved watching Sole' love something. Like she'd glow - I can't explain it. Thirty minutes of that and she was inquiring about my bedroom. Finally, it was time for her to see my favorite room of my castle. Walking past my gentlemen's mega lounge with the two-hundred-foot videogame wall, a plethora of bronze pieces of art and my wine cellar with the funky multicolored shag carpeting and abstract backsplash. A few feet up towards my highspeed, glass elevator which led us towards the upper level. I couldn't tell if she was impressed yet. We were finally at my bedroom which was located at the backend of my home - a dimly lit, clandestine late-night hangout that reeked of dusk til dawn evenings. Perimeter dripped in black and gold. My open-concept bedroom laced with floor-to-ceiling sliding glass doors that led to a marble patio and saltwater infinity pool. My place to unplug, reset my life, and take the time to be quiet and hear myself. My sanctuary. Skyline overseeing the city and ocean. Glass ceilings. Waterfall dripping into my infinity pool with the underwater sound system. Italian rare marble floors all throughout. Front and center, my California king. Couple feet away, some exercise equipment near a water wall. Double height-ceilings and abstract light fixtures. Wraparound balcony which dripped the other side of the perimeter of my room. Tiki torches strategically placed. The ambient lighting system that mimicked nature was sicko mode. She was blown away by the view. Not the intricate details, not my exotic plants or million-dollar trinkets and fixtures but the fuckin opulent view. Thee unorthodox Sole'. Her eyes glued to the view, I hit a button triggering my glass wall to blackout completely before converting into a wall of mirrors as now she was looking at herself.

"So what you been doing these days?" I broke the silence.

"You know me. A little bit of this. A little bit of that." She traced the walls with her fingertips. Her toes painted different colors. Blue, purple, pink, yellow, and orange.

"Still a feather in the wind I see. You still sporadically dance over at The Pearl?"

I inquired referring to a high-end strip club. Since I'd known her, she danced at a gentlemen's club once a month. Never enough to be called a stripper but just enough to be called a dancer if you get what I mean.

She said she did it to keep fit. Another time she said she did it because she got high off it. Back in the day, I felt she did it to spite her father. Today, I think she still does it to prove to herself that she'll always and forever be that girl. The one. The shit. The truth. Sole' had the aesthetics of Columbiana on the wake up but who she truly resembled was shawty off P Valley, the red joint – Autumn Night. She was built different. Back when she was mine, I'd pop up on her at the club and we'd role play like we were strangers, and she would go crazy off that shit. She'd make her quota, pay her bills and then we'd grab some Sonic. After that, we'd go back home to fuck and study….and sometimes argue.

"Twelve times a year. You know everything about me." She smiled, reapplying lip gloss.

"I know that you're vegan until you don't want to be. You dance until you don't feel like dancing. I won't even bring up your temporary love for baking. You lose interest quicker than any man I know." She ignored me, keeping it cool. "So besides reading books and staying fine, what you been up to?'

"I told you, a little bit of this and a little bit of that."

"Hmm, some things will never change."

"And what is that supposed to mean?" Unravelling one of her buns, half of her hair dripped down her left shoulder and breast. Her eyebrows perched up, prepared to be offended by my next statement.

"Nothing. You still look beautiful that's all."

Sole' blushed a little. "And you're still smooth with it. I'm not baking these days if that's what you're hinting at."

"Good. Could never cook for shit." Memories of her almost burning down our condo years back made me laugh. Another time in the dorm we shared with Markell. Fire extinguishers, a kitchen full of smoke. Yeah, just wasn't her creative niche.

"Well…. I haven't been baking." She restated, growing silent. "That's what I always hated about you."

"What you hate about me? The fact that you're a habitual quitter and I'm the only one that loves you enough to call you out on it?" I asked the ex-love of my life. She looked at me with that look that haunted me.

"Master of-none."

"Nah you're just a quitter."

Sole' was zoned out, focused on some peacock décor plastered on a nearby floating shelf until she faintly uttered, "I did love baking."

"I can't tell. You loved baking then you quit. Loved track. Quit. Loved acting, quit that. Loved law. Quit. Loved psychology, physics and broadcasting – quit. Loved me. Quit me. Track and field. Quit. Loved painting…"

"I NEVER QUIT PAINTING!!!" She yelped a bit as she was sexy when she was slighted and Sole', the real Sole' was in love with art. Art had her heart.

"That's real good. Always loved your paintings. Why'd you kiss me in my office?"

"You really think I'm a quitter?" There was pain in her eyes as I looked her square in them.

"Baby girl…..you're the biggest quitter I know."

"Welp." Sole' gulped hard followed by harsh silence. "I guess everyone can't be as focused and ambitious as *Prince Roberson*." A sarcastic grin coated her lips. "Where's your closet?"

"Nah you just use the word *love* loosely."

I pointed towards the huge walk-in closet, ignoring the fact that she bypassed my question. She undressed to change into my apparel as it was going to be a long fuckin night. She was in my closet, doing whatever her heart desired and my dick was harder than Chinese arithmetic.

"Thee Prince Roberson. I must say, I was expecting a far more elaborate closet." She popped her shit.

"I have another one on the other side of the house."

"Of course you do." A few minutes later, she came out naked with an oversized checkered suit jacket and a top hat.

"You like that one?" I smiled as she nodded doing her little dance on her tiptoes. She pranced towards me, her body just as beautiful as I left it so I reached to grab her.

"You crazy nigga? Sit back and enjoy your show." She pushed me backwards lightly with her foot as she crawled away. Giving me the perfect glimpse of that perfect ass. My fantasy fashion show.

"Can I at least tip you?" Three hundred singles collecting dust in my dresser drawer, weathered through my mind.

"This ain't The Pearl, plus money is the cheapest form of currency. What you can do is put on some Ro James."

She blew me a kiss as I watched her prance around my master suite in my suits. I changed the music as requested feeling like I was in a dream. Maybe I was just a pawn in her lucid dream. Yeah, that's what this was, had to be. Who cares? Long as I didn't wake up before I tapped dat ass. I was envisioning what I was going to do to her if she let me. Eyes glued. Senses heightened, I played it cool switching up the music again.

"Guess."

"Knowing you ex-boyfriend, D'Angelo."

She smiled as *Brown Sugar* floated through the room. She swayed her body like the girls from the music video, my brown sugar. *Lady* played next, reminiscing on the time she bought us tickets to the D'Angelo show at the Apollo Theatre – a very memorable birthday gift. A dick suck from the one you love on a dark orchestra balcony while *Me And Those Dreamin Eyes of Mine* flowed live from your favorite artist forever sticks with a nigga.

"Play *Nothing Even Matters*." Sole' instructed tiptoeing around my spot as I obliged. She loved that song. I loved watching her love that song.

"You still like getting your pussy ate from the back?" I zoomed in on the very thought.

"I never liked that. That was always a *you* thing." I had sex with her a million times, I knew what she liked but if she wanted to treat me like *new dick*, cool. Sporting a purple suit jacket now, she was crawling on the floor, admiring herself in my mirrors. Like she was getting high off herself in all those reflections as her hands traced her body. "You're a narcissist for having a million mirrors in your bedroom." She was now tiptoeing across my bed. Her eyes still glued to herself as she kept dancing, floating to the melodies. My muse. Least used to be.

"Ain't enough mirrors in this bitch wit ya conceited ass."

I removed my watch and jewelry, tossing them in a safe. She tossed the jacket on the floor, alongside the others to grab a cream jacket, no hat this time. Frizzbeeing the hat across the room, making a mess, she then began playing with my stripper poles.

"You're a dickhead for having three stripper poles. One not enough? Definitely a dickhead for fucking that big booty girl at the rooftop party knowing I'm there."

"That ain't got nothing to do with you."

"True."

She gave me a little show, spinning around my poles as I clapped twice altering the scenic lighting a bit. Red light special. A shattered glass designed blazer jacket draped her body as she created silhouettes with her body, spinning around and around like a carousel utilizing all three poles. I reminisced about when she used to let me play in all three holes. Sole' - my walking, talking contradiction. So beautiful. No one did it quite like Sole'.

"So what do you like?" Since she wanted to pretend like I wasn't in tune with her, I'd let her fake school a nigga.

"My favorite way to shut you up of course. Riding your face." She spun down a pole ethereal-like, now she was grinding on the floor, sorta like before. Biting her lips, rubbing on her body. She smiled that innocent smile and stopped all of a sudden. "Let's go swimming." Hopping up like a little kid, butt naked this time, I watched her dive into my seventy-foot wraparound infinity pool mermaid-like. I took my time as I couldn't believe she was here.

"You truly never stopped painting?" I asked this enchanted creature. She simply smiled and continued to swim.

"Why Prince?"

"It's just funny you're here and it's funny you still love painting. I'm starting up a tie line and I'd love for you to work your magic." Sole' stepped back and looked at me with new eyes. Then displayed a grin, followed by an eyeroll.

"Now you want to add me to your dreams."

"You always were a part of my dream. Always. If you need an excuse on why you up and left to New York then to Bali to *find yaself*, now back to LA, you're gonna have to find a sexier theory."

"Yeah." She grew quiet. "There are a million starving artists. You'll find someone to run your line."

"So you turning down my job offer? I pay well."

"I'm not here for a muthafukkin job Prince."

"Ight. What are you here for?" Question of the evening.

She politely hopped out the pool, grabbing a bottle of Don Perion on the way. A white robe was already awaiting her as I stayed put in my pool. Sole' opted to air dry, prancing around my place naked with impeccable confidence. The California air, my exotic plants and her dancer body were the perfect mix.

"You're the girl who can make a ten-dollar vintage crop top Tupac tee and distressed jeans look like a billion dollars. That's who you are."

"I'm a little more than that baby. You still anti-smoke?" She began rolling trees turning on some Lenny Kravitz' *Are You Gonna Go My Way*.

"No. Adderall, sleeping pills, a molly from time to time." I pointed towards my orange pill bottles on the counter. Finally let Dr. Swanson medicate a nigga.

"Let's swap vices."

She grabbed two of my pills and took them and then she handed me her blunt. I hadn't smoke since college, so I hesitated for a second before I lit it. She watched me swim as we cyphered a joint. My underwater thoughts – this is someone else's woman. Not mine. I kept forgetting about that part. Her legs dangled into the water as she watched me do a few laps. Back and forth, back and forth. Swimming up towards her feet, feeling better than I'd ever felt I decided it was time to kick up.

"Lay back."

I instructed as she inhaled weed, closed her eyes and obliged. Kissing her knees, I reached for a nearby ice bucket and traced the ice around her toes, ankles, calves and knees. Back and forth, up and down, circles around her legs as she tried not to squirm. Tossed the semi-evaporated ice into my mouth and began placing cold, sensual kisses on her knees and thighs while massaging her feet and ankles causing her breathing to intensify. Multi-stimulation as I was always a master at making Sole' lose her mind. Grabbing for her ass, she arched her back some more as I ate her pussy on the edge of my pool, ensuring she kept cumming. Spread that pussy apart and had that thang pulsating. She was loud, I was hungry and we both loved it. She scooted back, crawled towards me on all fours and slurped on my tongue. Grabbing my face, she slurped deep and then looked into my eyes.

"I'm proud of you."

She whispered placing her forehead on mine – something we used to do way back when we were in love. Then she hopped up and walked towards my living room. I followed her. Petrified she was going to disappear. So scared, I was on her like a magnet.

"Pretty flowers." She tiptoed past a bouquet of long stem red roses on a table.

"Shit they're yours." Shit, she could have anything she wanted for real.

"In retrospect, a dozen roses aren't romantic." Sole' tiptoed around my house admiring the art. I could think of a million women who felt otherwise, but I let her get her shit off.

"Oh yeah? What's romance then?" I quizzed as she picked one rose from the dozen and handed it to me. Then she kissed my hand.

"That's romantic. Simplicity."

"Says the most complex woman I know."

"*Simplicity is like a sycamore. Quiet, nude and living weather to the core. Its terseness speaks to me of skeletons. So tissue paper frail against the sun. I count the bare bones of emotion's dance. The glory and the pity of the circumstance. Lifts us to the apex of poverty. Where there is nothing but a need to be. Though sunset is a thread upon the hill and dying light severely tests the will. Just that we matter is of so much worth. We scarcely notice that it costs the Earth...*" Sole' twirled around like a ballerina. I think she was feeling my Adderall because I didn't know what the fuck she was talking about. I took back some alcohol, keeping my eyes glued on her.

"You like my home?"

Sole' smiled, her curly hair dripping down her back. "It's not bigger than Bill Murray's or anything. You still working on it or somethin?"

"Of course. You know my mind is always on the money." I knew she was being sarcastic and I always liked that about her.

"Yeah, I know. I'm glad you kept Markell close. He's the reason why you have this extreme success ya know."

"You're not going to give me any credit?"

"You're so so." Sole winked as Erykah Badu's *Other Side of the Game* pierced the room, fluttering off the walls. She swayed her body, arms in the air like strings in the wind. "So, you're financially free?"

"Why you need a loan?" I lit a few nearby candles.

"No."

"Yes I am financially free. Money will never be an issue. Ever baby." An eye roll was her response which was a strange response even for her. "What's that about?"

"Money isn't everything. It's great but it's not the end all to be all. Don't want you to get caught up in the fiction of a thing ya know."

I mean, wasn't she the one inquiring about my financial freedom? In that moment, I wanted to tell her about the visions. Wanted to confess that I couldn't stop thinking of her. That I saw her in every woman I encountered. In everything I did but I didn't want to scare her. Turning towards Sole' whose eyes had grown wide gawking at my Basquiat painting, her mouth dropped to the floor.

"Wow. Prince. Now I'm impressed." She powerwalked over towards the piece of art, gasping as if she had just run into Michael Jackson.

"You like it?"

"Like? I love it!!! I'm in Heaven. You better let me have it." Her eyes lit up like Christmas morning as she hugged my painting – the first time I'd seen her ecstatic all evening. I looked at her as if to say *bitch you must be crazy*. I may love you, shit may even be in love with you but I'm not a complete fool.

"You're too unpredictable. Nah. I'll give you a job creating my tie line and you can earn it but not my Basquiat. It was a gift. It's priceless."

"I respect that. Dope gift." She gave the piece of art one last look as I followed her back into the bedroom.

"You gonna let me finish eating your pussy?" I was too horny at this point and was tired of the games. She nodded her head, lighting another spliff. Then she grabbed for her drink. I politely took her drink and threw it on the floor. Glass splattered across my marble, I reached for her. "Come here." She shook her head no, walking backwards away from me with a playful grin.

"Sole', come here." I pulled her close. "What's up with your man?" She sucked her teeth, abruptly pulling away.

"The moon is full, the night is perfect, I'm naked and you have a fuckin Basquiat casually hanging in your hallway. I'm having the time of my life and I'm horny as fuck and out of all the things going on right now in this very moment, that's what you decide to ask me?"

She seemed a lil disappointed in my pimpin. She kept playing this cat and mouse shit, knowing damn well that I was going to go balls deep in that pussy. These fuckin cat and mouse games. She was just delaying the inevitable. I could hear her pussy calling me already. *Prince. Princeeee. I miss you. Stroke me out Prince.* Oh, I heard that pussy calling me. All this false power trippin was getting boring. Come let me take you down like old times, like present times, like forever times. My pussy. Most importantly, fucking Sole' would cure me permanently. I grabbed her fine ass and bust her down on the floor and then we made our way to the bed where I didn't plan to go but hey, we're here now. She sucked my dick real good and I returned the favor tenfold. Before I could finish, she pulled me up from bobbin for apples and demanded that I enter her. I could see in her eyes that she couldn't hold back so I obliged and damn it was good, just like I remembered it. I put her legs by her ears and stroked her into an oblivion. Grabbing her throat, I controlled her body and every orgasm for a while. She submitted as I melted into that pussy. Then she hopped on top and took herself to ecstasy. Jungle sex. I fucked Sole' like the world was ending tomorrow and I fell deeply in love all over again. One hardcore fuck, the second time we made love. Slurping on each other's tongues, I was gone. Recalling the day we fell in love, seven years ago. This Creole, genius, exotic creature. Our shit was love at first sight too. Queen Sole'. The unforgettable. The unfuckwitable. Unimaginable.

It was round three and I had crawled deep up in my ex-love like quicksand. Wasn't til about five strokes in when Ashley's beautiful face popped up in my mind. I hesitated for a moment but continued bustin Sole's ass. Ashley's big ole booty bouncing on my dick to Sole's slender body riding me like a cowgirl. It happened again when I was hittin it from the side. Flashes of Ashley then back to Sole'. Like a glitch. Brief. Super brief.

"You okay baby?" Sole' moaned as I got my head back in the game and got to work. I wanted her back, so I got my baby back. Wasn't long after that when we passed out into a deep like coma. I guess Ashley was my appetizer and Sole' was dinner. Charge that shit to the game.

8

devil's pie

Round four. Sole' had crawled on top of me and was riding my dick again except it was pitch black so all I saw was her silhouette, slipping swirling and sliding on me. That love drunk sex.

"I love you Prince."

"I love you too girl."

"And I love this dick."

"Oh I know you do." I controlled her hips as she rode slow.

"I hated fuckin Mike. He doesn't know my body. I had to fantasize about you to cum. What a tragedy." She confessed, hopping on her feet still riding. She's always been an acrobat.

"Oh yeah?" I dug deeper with a sedated grin, ego inflated like a blimp.

"Hell yeah!" She moaned real loud. "You know you're the best. You know what else baby? Of course I wanna run your tie line. You know I want to. You always know what I want." She purred confessing all her feelings. I just rubbed her clit while she rode this dick. "You think we can have the business and the romance and make it all work out? Make it all balance out Prince baby?" She moaned provocatively.

"I love you Sole'." I was so in love with this woman.

"Promise?"

"Yeah."

"I regret us breaking up baby. I couldn't stop dreaming of you." She whispered tears trickling down her face as she rode me slowly keeping her eyes locked on mine. Sole' moaned and splashed on my dick, pussy getting juicier and juicier. She began going faster and faster and then she slowed it back down before she leaned in close to me. I melted her body into mine. My baby, my love. Her lips near my ear, the sweetest kiss.

"Don't you get it? I own your fucking soul you stupid ass nigga."

She whispered in a demon like demeanor which triggered me to ferociously push her off me. I shook my head as it was morning. A nightmare. A fucking nightmare. Wasn't new to those. Probably my guilt for dissin Ashley. *Zoom* by The Commodores was skipping on vinyl when I awoke from that corny bullshit. Clock read 11:12. Discombobulated, I sat up anyway. Sole's side of the bed was empty, on the nightstand sat her prerolled joints and a hair tie. Proof she was actually here and this whole thing wasn't created from my dopamine induced memory. Was I surprised by her disappearance? Nah, I mean she was technically in a relationship with that corny dude from the party. Despite her genre of *crazy* she's ultimately a good girl and probably had to get back to her real life. Whatever the fuck that was. Probably playing house wit ole boy, ruining his life and shit. I didn't have to freak out. She'd be back. They always come back and if she wanted to demote herself to a casual smash, I'm wit it. She was someone else's headache for real. Pussy was good. Real good. Just how I left it. Anyway, back to reality.

Turning on my surveillance cameras so I could see her fine ass leave on the playback, I staggered over towards my monitors to study my ex. Enjoyed a bit of our sex session, I ain't even gonna hold you. Watched us sleep too. According to my surveillance, she crawled away from me around 4 am. That heart ass was pretty in black and white. She slipped her clothes on tiptoeing out, but she didn't leave emptyhanded. Nah, not alone. She took a souvenir. Plastered across my monitor, Sole' slippin my Basquiat painting off my wall and walking away. Thief ass bitch. Once she was at the door, she looked towards my camera and flipped me the bird. Both hands too. Then she blew me a kiss and she and my painting were in the wind. I rewound the footage about ten times, intaking the whole thing. Sitting on the edge of my bed, I grabbed one of her blunts and lit that bitch. Inhaling deep, I let the smoke marinate for a minute. Eyes shut, I exhaled. An elaborate puff of smoke. *What's to make of all of this?* I smoked another blunt and tossed this bitch's hair ribbon in the trash. Then I dialed up Ashley and of course she didn't answer. Pacing my room, housekeeping startled the shit outta me, I was so deeply caught up in my head.

"Should I come back?" Lydia asked meekly.

"Nah. I…Nah."

I brushed past her towards my kitchen to get a drink while she cleaned up and saged my home. Walking past my million-dollar mirror, I was clearly still that nigga and still had a multimillion-dollar business to run. My mind was wylin so I forwarded all appointments to their respective parties. Cleared my books and smoked. Three days I smoked and smoked and smoked as flashes of our sexual encounter roller-coastered through my brain. Aimlessly wandering my mansion in a daze attempting to wrap my mind around the whole thing. Lucid as shit. Sent Ashley some Chanel since bad bitches love Chanel – still radio silence. A pipe bursting ultimately flooding my basketball court didn't make shit any better. A few calls to maintenance for repairs alongside more calls to Ashley. Nothing. I was no good with a fucked up mental so to clear my head I was off to a private island. Maintenance would be doing the repairs so I was out. Yup. Fuck all of it. I'm rich ho.

"Markel. Hold everything down. I'm gone for a minute."

"More than a week?"

'I'm thinkin two or three maybe. I gotta get the fuck away." I emphasized to my right hand.

"Damn ight. Shit helicopter, yacht or jet?"

"Private."

"Say less. Peace brotha."

I'd come back fresh as new. This mission I had to tackle alone. Told Bianca to send Ashley a few dozen roses to her house and office before leaving Los Angeles. Hopping on my bike, I rode out towards my private airstrip just to think. Shit, I needed a vacation anyway. A real one. Few hours later I was coasting up towards eutopia. Yeah, I needed this. I sat on this captivating island sippin my favorite beer as *Roll Some Mo* by Lucky Daye glazed my eardrums. Called Ashley again to no avail. Then I called my little freak. Yup. Fuck it. My favorite lil Scorpio friend.

"Jessica. You feeling islandy?" My nickname for her was *Jessica Rabbit.*

"Whatever Prince. I'm always feelin islandy. Fly me out handsome."

She purred like the pro she was. Three hours later I was sipping pinacolatos with beautiful Jessica Rabbit. Partook in some soulful, beautiful conversations and then we went back to the villa and fucked. Hour after that we're at the tiki bar and Jessica Rabbit is handing me a piece of paper. My first NDA! I was shocked because this was my homie. Hit it numerous times in the past. Plus I give them, I don't get em.

"Scorpio. Trust issues."

Sensing my offensive energy she shrugged sweetly finishing up her jerk wings. Jessica Rabbit dipped a day later as I spent the remainder of my time in solitude. No women. Shit, that was my problem. Women. I loved women but damn! Then I started thinking. Did I treat women like disposable pleasures? Was I a shallow narcissist? I felt like a deep dude, so this was conflicting. When I'm by myself, I'm very profound. My truest essence. I mean, my relationships I had with the women in my family, my assistant Bianca, my sis Wanda Sykes, my staff (minus Maria) my peers, coworkers and the other numerous women in my life – they were different, fruitful, professional, noble. I felt like I treated women accordingly. If you're a queen, I treat you like a queen. Ashley was a play I fumbled - simple as that. But who was I as a man, for real? My mom didn't raise no obnoxious pig. Hell nah. She raised kings, both her and my dad. My dad was a wise street nigga and my mom was his loyal angel and they were big on men being kings. At least that was their aim. Looking down at my NDA, I was mortified again. Who the fuck did this bitch think I was? Then I started having regrets. Was I a fool to let Sole' get close to me again? Was I a mark for that shit? Sole' had always been fake diabolical as fuck. Underneath it, a sensitive, insecure, rebellious little girl way deep inside. I knew her but she knew me too. She could have the painting. Eat your heart out lil bitch. Maybe I could call Ashley and invite her out here to the villa. Shit, she may need a real vacation too. Now that I reflected more, Ashley's sex session at the party was good as shit!! Like good good. She had three times the ass. Three! Man, I was slippin! I looked towards the sun and said a prayer and then I dialed Ashley again. Silence. *Fuck!* I breathed as my head was beginning to pound. It wasn't one of the attacks where I envisioned my ex. No, this was just heavy pounding. I hadn't had one of those in a while so it caught me off guard. Clenching my teeth and fists, reminding myself to breathe, I held my chest ignoring the concerned looks on nearby patrons' faces. Hated to admit it but sometimes I wait in anticipation for the visions, the tirades. Distortion. My metaverse. Confusing what's real and what's not. Wondering when it was going to creep up and attack. Wondering if this was the day it would totally destroy me. The shit was disrupting my fuckin life and this time there was no visions, just the heaviest of poundings. Lightning bulbs through the brains. *Please God don't let me die by myself on this island.* Hunched over, I gave life, time. Pain never lasts forever. Breathed deep and exhaled and was still, eerily still and then I felt better. Reaching for my newfound habit marijuana, I took a puff and let it sit as it calmed my nerves. Exhaled and now I was lucid and peaceful, this was better. Much better. God I needed help as I couldn't keep livin like this.

The next few days were about solitude. Peace. It felt good. Couldn't help to think of creative ways to get Ashley back. I'd figure that part out. Right now the waves of the ocean were calming my spirit. My soul needed this. Deserved this shit. It was day five and my phone was blowing up like crazy which was strange because I'm off the grid, overseas. I ignored them all and just called Markell.

"Yo." I had a massage scheduled in an hour with something foreign and was fresh off some jet skis. I ain't have time for no fuck shit. I paid people to worry for me.

"You see the news?"

"I'm off the fuckin grid."

"It's your boy Chuck. Old ass got ransacked. He's been picked up by the feds. Some shit about embezzlement and falsified documents and Ponzi schemes. Got us looking nuts out here."

I just froze, intaking as much as possible. "Fuck you talking about Markell? I'm not in the states right now." I rubbed my temples remaining calm.

"Man get back to LA!" *Bang.*

Packing my shit in a daze, I dialed my pilot and ignored all phone calls. I'd just tossed back some

Adderall so all this shit was bad timing. My heart was beating out my chest as I attempted to pack my shit and get the fuck back home. At least that was the aim. My fuckin accounts were frozen. *My* accounts. Frozen! Prince Roberson of Prince Apparel! Oh that's when I lost it. After about forty-five minutes of going ape shit, I calmed down. Told my pilot I couldn't pay him and twenty minutes later I was flying commercial, something I hadn't done in a very long time. I could've called people for help but I was ashamed and pissed. I probably should have because I'd forgotten about the paparazzi. Cameras in my face, microphones and flashes, I powerwalked towards my terminal keeping my head low ignoring questions of Chuck. Zipping up my coat, I made my way through the hectic airport.

"Prince! A comment!"

A random reporter screamed out as I brushed past her nosy ass, skipping down the escalator stairs the opposite way looking like a madman zipping through the airport. High out my fuckin mind. Finally seated in my basic economy seat I made my flight by the skin of my teeth. Now I was jittering off the Adderall, fury drenched and mind in a daze. Shit, I wanted to cry word up so I just broke down and dialed my mom.

"Son."

"Ma….I love you ma."

"I know baby. I called you to ask why you missed church again but I can't even do that. I saw the news. You been praying baby?" I hadn't and that was the truth. Hadn't seen the news and hadn't been praying. I'd look at that shit when I got to LA.

"I will ma. I will."

"Yes you will. I love you son. Stay sucker free son. You keeping your hands clean?"

"Squeaky clean ma. I promise."

"Ok baby. Do not let them demote you from a king to a pawn. Don't get swiped off your board. This is your board. You hear me Prince?"

"I hear you ma."

"I'm praying for you. Both you and my bonus son Markell. I don't know the other three that good and I don't know if Chuck is innocent or not but all five of you are in my prayers. Especially you. I love you."

What I needed to hear. Long as my momma loved me, things weren't so bad. We finally landed to LA as I brushed past all the common folk and I was embarrassed about the whole thing. Didn't want anyone to see me on that flight. Bigger than that, I had to see what the fuck Chuck did to put everything on tilt the way it was. I called Markell back immediately once I got to LA.

"I'm at LAX. Why the fuck are the accounts frozen?"

"Nigga I ain't accounting! Prince I'm stuck at Home Depot with a cart full of shit and a frozen black card. Paparazzi swarmed outside like fuckin roaches. They're everywhere so I'M asking YOU why are the accounts frozen?" Markell countered as Chuck had obviously done some real live bullshit.

"Yo call Omar." Markell dialed Omar to no avail as I tried not to lose my shit again. "Call Lyle." Markell dialed Lyle and he picked up.

"Bro, what the fuck."

"Chuck locked up?"

"Yeah, but fuck that gotta do with us? Do you get that *my* accounts are frozen? Muthafukkas are outside both of my homes. My wife is freaked out. I'm trying to convince my other wife from filing for divorce. They on my property and shit. I got kids!" Lyle sounded confused and pissed.

"I'ma kill Chuck." I blurted enraged. "Look, don't say shit. Ain't no story to fuckin tell. Lay low in your lavish fuckin mansions and be cool. Act normal. Stay the fuck out the press."

"You expect us to sit here in the fog with no clarity and how do we know if our lines are bugged? They hittin Chuck wit a RICO! A RICO Prince. Not to mention there's a Ponzi scheme meme floating around the web with our faces! The internet is unmatched my nigga. My lawyer said not to speak to anyone from Prince Apparel until this is lifted and I don't want any additional issues man. Have your attorney reach out if you really need me ight? Hold ya heads." Lyle stated before he ended the call.

"My lawyer said the same shit." Markell added as my lawyer was one of many people blowing up my phone.

"Fuck that. Call Omar back." I was steaming hot livid as Omar didn't answer again.

"He's probably following his lawyer's advice."

"Call him again." I requested through clenched teeth in a much calmer tone. Five more outbound calls to Omar - silence.

"Donyale is calling me. I'll hit you later. Go home and relax. I gotta explain this shit to my wife." Markell ended the call as I took a Lyft home.

What the fuck was going on? Doing some deep reevaluating at this point, I was trying to grasp what happened. I went from having this flawless time with this queen, Ashley that is, to being sucked into Sole's bullshit once again. Ashley cured me already so how did I get sucked into Sole's shit again? How? It's like the shit happened so fast. I was already fuckin happy. I already won. Man listen! Now my whole world felt like it was going to shit. What the fuck was happening right now? Better yet, attempting to happen because I wasn't crashing out like that. Over my dead body.

It was coming to the point to where I was anxious of when my next mental tirade would arise. I'd time them out – one every three hours about. Sometimes five, sometimes seven but sometimes they'd come back-to-back followed by days when they didn't come at all. The whole shit made me anxious, overwhelmed and stressed and it was no way for a man to live. I really wanted to sleep away the pain my heart was feeling. Still hadn't gotten all the details about Chuck's bullshit. All I heard was indictment, frozen accounts, embezzlement, RICO and the FBI. All I needed to hear. Kept envisioning them kicking down my doors and taking me away too. I'm black in America, they don't really need a reason. Then the news of my employees' checks bouncing started circulating as my own staff couldn't pay their bills. All ricocheting from my accountant being a fraudulent lying snake. It was my job to know he was going to fuck me. Why hadn't I seen this shit coming? Chuck of all people fuckin *me* over! Me being a firm believer of thoroughly reading the room, my personal quote is if you can't spot the sucker at the table it's usually you. Chuck fuckin played me. Made a sucker outta me. My employees being affected could tarnish my good name and brand so I'd pay them out of pocket, no doubt but the shit was fuckin with me. Draining as shit and really really fuckin with me! After another Adderall, some alcohol and weed, I power walked towards my basketball court instantly feeling water on my shoes. Before I knew it, I was on the ground. *Splat!* I was out.

Waking up gazing towards the ceiling with blurry vision, I eventually realized I was on the floor of my gym. Attempting to focus in on the clock plastered across my scoreboard, I see that hours had gone by. Peeling myself off the ground, I reached for the back of my head which was throbbing with a sharp pain. Blood on my hands, I headed towards my bathroom avoiding the excess water around me. I hadn't paid maintenance to complete the job from the pipe bust. On my head, a slight bruise and lump from the fall which wasn't so bad, I could deal with it. What I couldn't deal with was someone smiling in my face and playing with my money. Fury filled me all over again as I zoomed in towards my phone, a message from my attorney Frank screaming out *the accounts will be unfrozen soon* as if I was supposed to give a fuck. Like it mattered now. Shouldn't have been frozen in the first place. I staggered past my basketball court and grabbed some towels from a linen closet. Tossing them on my floor, ensuring I didn't slip again, I headed towards my elevator to my room. Finally mustered up the courage to read what they were saying about my company online and it wasn't good. Yeah, I was gonna kill Chuck. Reminding myself to breathe I ignored all three of my ringing phones, opting to call Ashley instead - still nothing. *Damn, Ashley sweetheart. Damn.* I yearned for some more rest but Sole' had been haunting my sleep for such a long time, a fact I'd been afraid to admit out loud to anyone. It was embarrassing. I had the option to go to sleep and have nightmares of my ex or stay awake and have visions. Life choices. I named them hyper dreams. Decisions decisions. Sometimes I could manipulate the daytime ones which is why I chose to stay up. The hallucinations were kicking up though. Intensifying. I'd see her in the mirrors. In raindrops. Situations and scenarios. A glass of wine. My waterfall. A piece of art. Even catching the eye of a random woman would link me back to her. An item will trigger me to think of her. Sometimes nice and sometimes nasty. My life revolved around my ex-girlfriend and the shit was unpleasant. Very unplaya. She lived in my dreams. Lived in my mind rent free. I kept my cards close to my chest because it sounded like some weak ass shit to be going through and I didn't want to sound crazy. On top of that, I'd have flashes where the right side of my face would temporarily go numb. Couldn't pinpoint what that shit was about. Lightning flashes of waves shot through my brain, down my spine through my nervous system causing me to hunch over off a reflex. Head bowed, eyes closed, I waited for it to stop. It eventually stopped. Pacing my mansion back and forth trying not to lose my mind, I acquired five hours of sleep in forty-eight hours. I was surrounded by luxury so fuck it, right? Yeah….a theory I was trying to marry but I just couldn't. Felt like who I truly was at my core wasn't who I was portraying. Sometimes the things I evoked threw me off and I'm me! Like if I could see myself on the playback, I'd be appalled and I'm the one running my life. I'm the one orchestrating my plays. Right? Well, was I? I was rich that's for sure. The one responsible for the money, the checks. The fuckin checks!! Thoughts of my accountant Chuck fucking me over infuriated me as I was triggered all over again. My phones were on DND and I was pissed. It was two nights later when Markell hit me. I had just had comatose sex with some nameless woman, a Jane Doe. Anything to avoid the tabloids. Anything to avoid the fact that Ashley was gone. Walking past my bare wall where my Basquiat used to hang, I walked back towards my despair chair. I was two hours into a sunken dreary daze when I accidentally answered my best friend's facetime. I ain't feel like talkin for real.

"Prince."

"Yeah man."

"We going out tonight. Shake that shit off, fix ya face. Do I have to pull up on you? You're not answering your phone. You treating me like some *random*."

"I'm fucked up."

"Trust me. Come out."

I sighed deep, staying put for a moment. "Personal or business?"

"Both but mostly business like you prefer. All the shit you like."

"How the fuck you so calm right now?" I reached towards my last blunt.

"I'm not. You're just so manic that I gotta act calm even though I'm really shittin bricks. You ain't leave a nigga no room to freak out. That and I have a successful wife, so. Wasn't for Donnie I'd be trippin. They're unfreezing the accounts this week so we going to be ight. You gotta know that. Shit we legit, fuck Chuck."

"I'm not well bro."

"I know you're not. Look this is what the fuck you're gonna do." He pointed at me as if he was trying to break his finger through the screen. "You're gonna get ya ass in that bathroom and hop in that water, then you're gonna get fly in one of them dope ass suits, put it all together and we're going out. Let's have some fun and do what we do because no one does it like we do. Nobody. You hear me?"

I'm instantly inspired listening to my best friend whose always there for me even when I'm not always there for him. Least I could do was get out of bed. I got myself up and went to go watch Sole's footage again. Watched that shit fifty times in a loop. The sadness of Janet Jackson in Poetic Justice when she's eating the popcorn with the hot sauce, yeah that sad shit lingered through my mansion. Sole' loved Poetic Justice, her third favorite movie. Eves Bayou's her second. Yeah, I needed to get out this house. Markell pulled up at 8 and we were off as I opted to keep my women trouble to myself. We had bigger fish to fry.

"Look. It's looking bad for us right now but it's ALL good because we some raw niggas from the gutter so this ain't shit, feel me?" Markel was in rare form. I mean it was crunch time and my energy wasn't very leaderlike lately.

"Omar still isn't answering." I clenched my fists, reminding myself to breathe.

"That nigga gonna hit you when the accounts are unfrozen. Don't worry about that. Prince Apparel is going to survive this shit show. Tonight, we're going into this fundraiser like kings, like this scandal Chuck got us in ain't doing shit to our confidence. We're not done. We're just getting started really. You hear me bro?"

"Yeah man." I sat up in my seat. I was too real to fake it, but I could make a good attempt. My spirit was disarray but not fucked up enough to just give up on my business.

"Lil Baby is the next hot thing and if we can get him to rock our shit, we in there. Won't matter if our accountant is on some bullshit. We gotta keep it pushing. Gotta keep our faces out there. This is the industry we chose. Lil Baby's big on energy and nonprofit and giving back. Business as usual."

I fixed my tie and posture, taking it all in displaying new confidence. "By the end of the night, all them muthafukkas gonna be rocking Prince Apparel."

"That's what I'm talking about! That's the Prince I fuckin know."

Markel clapped his hands wildly as if his favorite sports team was winning. He was good at hyping me up. Reminded me of back in the day when he would have to shake me out of my rut, forcing me to get out of my own way. Forty-five minutes later, we're boarding Lil Baby's Lamborghini yacht – the supercar of the sea. His shit was insane. Put any yacht I'd seen before to shame. I slid in behind Markell, keeping my cool. Saw a few familiar faces, keeping everything brief for obvious reasons. Markell was shaking hands, keeping it suave and smooth and things were lookin alright.

"We love you Prince and Markell. They can't keep the black man down!"

Someone yelled out from a crowd of faces. We kept it cool. Markell walked straight towards Lil Baby who was standing next to something fine as hell, brown, glossy, petite - probably his woman. Him and Markell conversed a bit and then we were introduced. Discussed a bit of business after he told me he apologized for what was attempting to happen to my company and hoped I was keeping my faith strong. I appreciated that. Chopped it up for about five minutes. After that, he politely turned down my offer. He shook my hand, told Markell to hit him and that was that.

"Rejection. Nice." I faced the sea and lit the last of my blunt.

"Nigga, when the *fuck* did you start smoking?!"

I just ignored him and puffed as he was worried about the wrong shit. Caught off guard, Markell gazed at me like I had three heads for about twenty seconds, shrugged and pulled out a few blunts easing into the new reality. *It is what it is* was his expression. I grabbed three of his nine joints, remaining silent as I cyphered a blunt with Markell. Inhaling deep, I let the smoke marinate for a moment as at this point I was an expert chiefer. Both our phones were going off at the same time, an email from Chuck's lawyer claiming his innocence which I ignored. Markell read over the details before putting his phone away. He could read the room because I ain't have shit to say. A side eye and head nod initiated the walk towards the corner of the yacht so we could really talk.

"Associating my name with a fuckin Ponzi scheme Markell. Shit got me boiling hot."

"Chuck got us in some bullshit – so what." Markell inhaled deep. "That's some Prince shit to say right? *So what*! Maria pregnant. *So what*. Prince you lost a quarter million at the Bellagio. *So what*. Prince, take it easy with these women. *So what*! That's someone else's woman Prince. *So what*! Prince, the waiter can't fill your cup up anymore, it's already to the brim. *I want more! So what*! That's ya new name nigga. *So muthafukkin what*."

Looking at my boy, I burst out laughing because it sure did sound like me, I couldn't front. I needed that laugh as we just smoked enjoying the scenery.

"You think I'm a lunatic man?"

"Hell yeah. I'm a little crazy myself though. Comes with the assignment. We both have big assignments man." Markell knowing me so well could sense I was having deeper personal issues. "How you really feelin bro?"

"I'm ight. Just facing a lot of components. A lot of side swipes. Like there's a shift going on and I can't grasp it."

"Maybe it's a positive shift." Markell blew out smoke.

"Nah, it's not positive."

"Well words are power. We gotta mind what we manifest. Your mom taught us that." Markell didn't have a family setting growing up. Shit, neither did I for real but Markell was in the foster system, so he'd come to my house for a hot plate making him my bonus brother. Anything beat that crazy foster lady Markell lived with. Twelve kids in a tiny three bedroom. Rapes, assaults, murders, yeah the foster system was all types of fucked up so Markell found comfort coming to my crib. My dad was in the streets but I always had my mom and I didn't mind sharing my momma with Markell. Her heart was big enough for everybody.

"True indeed."

"Maybe Maria keeping the baby is a good thing. Kids change people." See now Markell was fuckin trippin.

"She got rid of it."

"Word? Ok, silver lining. Silver lining! I was thinking I was about to be an uncle and shit."

I just laughed at my boy, feelin high as shit.

"She got a nice payout."

"Was it worth it?"

"One hundred grand for some pussy?" Ruminations of Maria's pretty ass bouncing on my dick made me smirk. "Semi."

"That's some pricey pussy. Hope you both learned yall lusty lesson. Oh yeah, Donnie wants to double date with you and Ashley again. It'll be smooth. I dig her for you. You looked happy wit her."

"Sole' is still fucking with my head." I finally admitted out loud.

"I don't know why. She ain't even your finest ex."

"Ha."

"For real and never forget, Prince Apparel popped way after she left you in the wind."

"What's your take on Sole'?" I inquired as Markell rolled more weed.

"Sole' DuBois? I mean, she was sis back in the day off the strength of you. She's a caveat. Cool but in the fuckin way. Ostentatious. Had a takeover spirit but she was tolerable plus you loved her so fuck it. She said she didn't want shit to do with the company which was the dumbest shit I ever heard. She can kick herself in the ass for making that bad business decision. Since we're talking about it, you were real selfish back in college having her stay in the dorm. I ain't outwardly complain because I was always in Rachel's dorm but still and all. Self-preserving Prince." Markell enjoyed the herb and the vent session as it was interesting hearing a perspective of my ex from a logical stance. "Self-preserving ain't always a bad thing though. Don't forget that part. That quality is what makes you the goat. Makes you the best."

"I fucked her." I hit the blunt and passed it to my mans.

"Rachel?"

"Sole'."

"Recently? Why nigga? Why! She was just with the Asian dude at Karl's party."

"Yeah I know. On top of that, she stole my Basquiat on the way out."

"What! Word?"

"Word."

"The *Basquiat* Basquiat?" A priceless painting Daisy gifted me in her will before she passed away.

"Evil man."

"Let me get this straight. She seduced you, fucked your brains out and then stole your shit?"

"Verbatim my nigga."

"That's what you get for letting her back in. Man, you're a good one because I would've hawked her down. That painting's worth more than her life."

"That part."

"Prince she's today's paper, yesterday's news." Markell passed me the blunt. "Yo, remember that night at Donnie's? The night I was giving you smoke about the twins?"

"Yeah, I remember."

"I wasn't mad at you for real. You caught me during an internal struggle. Them twins was fine as fuck. I had to go in the car and pray my guy. This faithful, married life thing ain't always that easy. Sometimes I envy your freedom. Rarely but it happens."

"Nah, I was wrong and you ain't missin shit. Donnie would fuck me up if she knew about that. I ain't shit man." I shook my head, a little disgusted in my behavior at times.

"Love you bro. You're a good person. Your goddaughters love you. Your fans love you. Our employees love you. The women love you too much. You ain't so bad bro." Markell passed me a blunt, showing love. I needed that.

"Them freezing the accounts scared the shit out of me. Made me feel like we were going broke. Start of a nigga's decline and shit."

"What's your version of broke though?"

I didn't want to think about that shit anymore as I hated broke thoughts. "I'm simplifying the company. Vote someone off. I vote Omar. I don't give a fuck what Chuck did or didn't do." Smoke circles from my mouth, I was higher than a giraffe's ass.

"Damn. Word? Like that?"

"Only people we need is each other for real. Everyone else was always disposable. Vote."

"I was looking forward to the quintet, us five coming back together. Damn let me think. I mean if we are voting, shit....Chuck for obvious reasons."

"Good. Lyle stays. Just us three. We never needed two lawyers and we can find another numbers guy." I finalized my decision.

"Prince off the trees is *that nigga*. I still can't believe I'm watching you smoke! Let's eat up this food and blow this gas." Markell patted me on the back as we headed towards the festivities. "Give Ashley time. She seems worth it. You just gotta sacrifice something."

"What are you talking about now Markell?" I bit into some shrimp.

"I'm saying, life is about sacrifice. For instance, if I were you I'd sacrifice gambling."

This fool was clearly high because I had my good eye on the crap tables on the upper level of the yacht over near the grand piano but I heard him. He was better off suggesting me sacrificing pussy. Ha, sacrifice. Man, maybe. *Feel Like Making Love* the Roberta Flack rendition painted a picture between my ears of times when things were oh so simple. The melodies whispered through the air from the second floor – my next stop. Then I started thinking about sacrifice. If it could bring Prince Apparel back to its highest elevation and Ashley back, man maybe. I called Ashley and she answered. She fuckin answered! Barging away from the crowd, a little nervous but still poised as ever as I focused in on my call. I had three minutes until they were kicking up speed and the Lambo yacht would be floating through the ocean at full speed, 60 knots. This call had to be quick.

"Ashley. Sweetheart."

She was quiet. "Work shit? Really Prince."

"Work shit. I swear. You seen the news. I been stressed over that. You see what your cousin did." The lies flowed from my mouth.

"That has nothing to do with me and you cut me off before that."

"I miss you." She didn't sound angry which was calming. She missed me too.

"I don't trust you."

Shit, now I was quiet. "I get that."

"Thank you for the flowers."

"What about the Chanel bags?"

"I owned all of them already so I sold them."

"I need to see you." I never begged but shit.

"I don't forgive you."

"Huh?"

"I don't forgive you because there isn't an apology."

"I apologize."

"Well…I don't forgive you."

"Why not?"

"Because. Because I feel like you're not telling me the truth." She hid her disappointment as I needed her to forgive me, for real. She was the source to my alignment. I didn't really deserve her.

"I love you Ashley and I apologize sincerely." Desperate measures and I needed her and fuck it, I did love her. I think I did. Had to as she played a significant role in my survival, my mental peace, my upward mobility.

"Now you love me."

"I do."

"You know what hurts my feelings most? I have sex with you and then you disappear. Then you try to pick me back up like I'm a yo-yo or something. On top of that, I wanted to present you the NBA contract the night we were supposed to have our special night but….." She grew quiet.

"What contract?"

"I had pulled some strings to get Prince Apparel a meeting for a contract with the NBA and wanted to surprise you. This was before you ghosted me and the Chuck allegations stuff." She mentioned sweetly, sniffling a little. Damn. I really wasn't shit. She was out here moving like a noble wife. NBA contract? You know how hard it is to get a NBA contract? Like the NBA rocking my shit exclusively? *Damn girl* is all I could utter.

"On top of that. I just kept having visions of you making love to somebody else over and over and over again."

"That's not what happened."

"Whatever. I can tell when you're lying."

"Look I'm sorry Ashley. I should've handled you better, work shit or not. Look, I'm over on Lil Baby's Lambo yacht, who just rejected doing business with me by the way. I'm taking Ls left and right. My business is going to shit in real-time because of your cousin but I'm happy because you finally answered my call. I'm finally happy. This is happy. Gimme a chance to show you something new. I don't fumble twice."

"I hear you Prince. I'll hit you later regarding business. Personal, I don't know about that. Tell Donnie hello."

Her energy exuded a woman who's trust I'd broken but at least I tried and more importantly at least she answered. After she hung up I felt a slight slither of hope. I didn't even go to the second floor to gamble. Nah, just kicked back and enjoyed the band and breeze. Now I could enjoy this yacht. Sixty-three feet in length, vessel made of carbon fiber, lounge version with the penthouse layout. Markell had his eye on the Bugatti yacht, so he was wrapped into all the details of the evening. This was one bullet shaped beauty. I didn't solidify any business that night but I felt peace which is priceless. I had one slight vision of Sole' but I eased through it and that wasn't so awful. Markell was chillen with Lil Baby for the rest of the night. That wasn't so bad, being left out. My boy looked good out there, moving and shaking. Probably convincing him to change his mind on Prince Apparel business. Best of all, Ashley answered. Fuck gambling. My pure girl was easing back towards me. My true one. Genuine. Sincere. A true queen. My good luck charm. Markell dropped me home with some weed and positive affirmations. Incense too, his wife's collection. Emphasized that just being at the party tonight and taking pictures with Lil Baby evokes a message. The power was in the details and Prince Apparel getting out this hole may be a slow burn but it wasn't impossible. We had the power to change the narrative. Maybe even use it to our advantage.

Smoke clouds all around allowing my thoughts to become clearer while I tried to make sense of everything that had transpired. Then my boy was off to his family. I came home and got in the pool, attempting to ease my mind with a swim. Thoughts of Ashley simmered my anxiety better than any form of self-medication. Ashley was freedom. Maybe tonight I'd get some good sleep. Maybe. Shit, sacrifice is powerful.

9

send it on

The next morning Ashley shot me a text sweetly requesting my time as I was intrigued all over again. I was lay up with something sexy and soft but I scooted over and zoomed in on my message. The text stated she heard I was in hiding and simply wanted to reach out. Told me she'd always be there for me before offering to take me out to lunch. The same spot we went to on our first date. A simple quiet lunch over the water, exactly what my soul craved. I opted to tell her the raw truth about everything regarding my ex and oddly enough, she respected it. Said she loved me for the transparency and would pray and fast for me. We vowed to have no more secrets and to work on our friendship. It felt good. The result of this lunch put me deep in thought. Like she pulled my coat, reminding me of who I was. An epiphany perhaps. I understood her perspective and it caused me to reflect on how I treated her and all women, for real. I needed to reevaluate how I moved. I treated them like shit and now that my dick was in the dirt, I could finally see clear. Vowing to do better and in the spirit of honesty, I started with my therapist Lisa. I called her out of the blue, confessing everything to her detail by detail. Told her how I lied to her and manipulated every session we had. How I sexualized each time we met. She listened.

"Prince. I emailed you. I'm not your therapist anymore."

"Why?" Confusion coated my face.

"Call the agency but I'm not involved. Good luck." Lisa was gone. Ahh so what. Tossing back three sleeping pills, I was gone too.

I woke up in fuckin Yonkers. Yonkers! How I got there I'm unclear, I was in Yonkers nonetheless. Scoping the perimeter, I was no longer in Los Angeles, but indeed back in the hood. Dusty rags dripped my body and I didn't recognize myself. Searching my pockets for my phone, wallet, keys, a handkerchief, a tie, watch, any symptom or glimmer of my real life – nothing. To the right of me, my big brother Bruce. Two dirty quarters in my hand. I began to freak out.

"What you looking for Prince?"

I was mute, looking up at my twin brother who still smelled like shit. My words were void and I reeked of shit and piss as well.

"We gonna eat soon. Just chill, stop crying crybaby."

Looking towards a piece of glass at my reflection, I couldn't fathom what the fuck was staring back at me. It was me but in the bummiest of rags. Nose snotty, skin blotchy, body weak, eyes yellow. My veins – I couldn't explain my veins. I clung to Bruce, my safety zone.

"Ahh Prince, move. Sit still." Bruce instructed as I tried to move my mouth again but I was comatose. "Don't you hate dad?" A conversation Bruce and I never had before in any lifetime.

"Don't say that!" I could finally speak.

"He's dangerous and spooky. You hear what they say about him in the streets. He's reckless. He's going to get us killed, all of us. Me. You. Mom. The dog. All of us. You pussy boy for not admitting you hate him too."

Tears dripped down my face as my legs couldn't move and mouth was muted again. Couldn't run, couldn't speak. The thought of something bad happening to my mom broke my heart and the way Bruce casually tossed the ideal out there killed me.

"Let's get some horse."

A sinister grinned plastered Bruce's face as he grabbed my arm and led me towards a dark alley. My legs seemed to be dangling in the air, I was floating. Like he was flying a kite. No weight, just Bruce's leadership. I followed him towards doom like maggots on shit. He was big bum and I was baby bum and he was calling all the plays. My money. My fuckin money! Where was my money? Where was my money? Where was it?! Didn't matter. Two dirty quarters was my new reality. Bruce was a feen and I was a feen too. I was a feen too!! A fuckin drug addict just like my fuckin twin!!! Me?? Nooooooo!!!!!!!! That's how I felt and internally plead but what I actually did was reach out to use a Prince Apparel tie to wrap my arm while Bruce played nurse and plucked the dirty needle. Rats towards my feet, a dumpster to the left of me, ten feens scattered amidst. Toothless zombies and I was right at home. Long as I had Bruce - right? My muthafukkin twin; the relationship I always desired, *voila*. The devil's potion trickled through my veins taking me to my new place of solitude, I was gone and it was over for me. No coming back. Game over.

I woke up back in bed and immediately checked my accounts. Then I checked my arms for marks, particularly my veins. Then my accounts again. A fucked-up nightmare. Out of breath as shit, I looked around as I was back in my mansion in my California king. What a nightmare! In the mirror I could see the hurt and pain of the demons I had dealt with. So much suppressed pain. Man listen. I know I told Markell I was going to sacrifice gambling but fuck that. Shit, the woman I'm sacrificing it for is a gambler! The accounts were unfrozen, so I texted Lyle asking if he wanted to hit the Bellagio. He was already there which revved me up as it was time to flip some fuckin money. I had access to my millions, Prince Apparel was midway through the hit and I was feeling lucky. Got some pussy real quick and then was off to Vegas.

Gambling is about saying *fuck you* to reality and defying the odds. Me being an expert at this shit, never thought about the odds. Welcome to the house of addiction muthafukkas. Movie stars, athletes, millionaires, business titans, amongst others graced the table. All chips stacked. White boy across the table was poppin his shit. Playing with his trust fund, his daddy's money. Probably never worked a day in his life. *Gimme dat.* I knocked his head off. Could slow walk him all night but I didn't have that type of time so I finished him off. He was tossing chips like a toddler at the loss. Russian muthafukka next to him raised the two million he knew he didn't have, spewing fake confidence. Got him too. You see, I was the only black face at the table and in my colorful mind, these fools owed me reparations and I was here to collect. Hours passed as the game fluctuated a bit. Something sexy slithered in sporting a pink mini dress. She kissed player three on the forehead and took a seat nearby. She looked like Sole'. I kept my eyes on the cards. *All in. No wait.* Player five tossed his keys in the pot. Memories of the night I won my yacht flurried through my mind. A serene smile coated my face as my phone rang.

"What's up?"

"Hey it's Ashley."

"I'm gambling sweetheart." Her voice was so pretty to me.

"Sorry for interrupting, get all the money. I was just calling you about meeting with the head chairmen next Friday but focus in on your game babe." This woman was pure gold.

"Come to Aruba with me." I could feel her smile through the phone.

"Okay. I will." Ashley blew me a kiss and hung up as I focused back in.

Player four was playing the odds and was up a bit but not for long. I won the next two, pushing me up a sexy four million! Bluffed off the win by yours truly. Three hours later, I was now up two million. Player three was now making his chips rain. I despised a premature winner which is why I knocked his head off next. By midnight I had quadrupled my buy in as I was the best player at most tables. Four million pushed into the pot. Stiff hands, proof of a bluff. Rookie was over there over betting, clearly anticipating the call. My head was on swivel. Everything came off the rip during one hand though. The beginning of my full tilt. I tossed in the winning hand as the rookie sitting across me had nothing. How had I known he had nothing? He accidentally flipped his card over. Exposed. The spot was blown as the me, the arrogant black guy who'd been kickin ass for years had finally lost to a fuckin amateur. The crowd was clapping as the rookie had been losing for weeks. I jumped back in sweating profusely this time, clearly off my game. Ego bruised, a lot of machismo. I was up one million and then down six million and that fluctuated like a seesaw, but I wasn't letting up. Fuck that. Grind that shit out. My phones were ringing like crazy again.

"Yeah?"

"A la mierda perra. Vete a la mierda. Crees que puedes tratarme como a una puta. Me quedo con el bebé!"

"The fuck?"

"Fuck you!" *Bang!*

I ignored that shit, focusing back in on the game and it wasn't long until my phone was ringing again.

"Fuck you want?!!"

"Prince, son it's me. Your mother."

"Mom. My bad ma, what's wrong?"

"Nothing."

"You're not telling the truth, I can hear it in your voice. Talk to me." I finally let my eyes off the cards.

"The cancer, son. They found traces."

My heart dropped to the floor but I internalized it. "You okay?"

"I'm great. I have an appointment next week and I want you to come with me."

"Anything you want. Anything. Of course."

"Okay baby. Love you."

"I love you more."

I hung up the phone with tears in my eyes and attempted to get my mind right as the Sole' lookalike in the pink dress sashayed out of the spot with a smirk. Phones were ringing again but I ignored it until I couldn't any longer. Shit, it could've been my mother.

"Yes ma!"

"Don't *ma* me. Send me some more money!" It wasn't my mom, but Maria again with the bullshit.

"Bitch, I paid you off. You're dead to me."

"Yeah yeah, I'm past all that. The money Prince. Take care of your responsibilities as a man and father!"

I hung up on the ho because she was getting me hot and this wasn't the time. My phone was going crazy yet again, attempting to throw me further off my game so I answered it one final time before I'd turn it off.

"Listen you slut bitch. I fucked you and nutted in you like the cum bucket you are. So what. I paid you to get rid of the baby, one hundred twenty-five Gs. If you blew through that shit already, fuck you. It's not my baby. Drink bleach bitch."

"Prince, it's me…. Ashley."

Pure shock. I'm usually good at adapting to any environment, scenario or situation but I had nothing. I apologized profusely, talking in circles but my words fell on deaf ears.

"Delete my number. Goodbye."

I was blocked again and it was over. She was gone. No getting her back this time. No NBA meeting. Eleven million in the hole after two days of losing. How could I get myself in such a dark hole? How could I lose the girl again? Maybe I subconsciously didn't truly want her. Maybe God was protecting her from me. Muthafukkas I'd been cleaning out for years were coming in taking my money. Some flying in.! My pride wouldn't let me see that everyone at the table was fucking me over in rotation, no pillow. Even the dealer was getting off. I stayed put, ready to gamble it all. Out of the corner of my eyes I spotted the last nigga on Earth I'd think to see. Omar dripped down in a Gucci suit, a woman on his arm. Not Sanaa either. This bitch ass nigga hadn't called me in weeks and here he was at the casino with some pussy. Peeling myself out of my seat, I strolled towards my ex-employee.

"Yo, O."

"Sup." Omar looked towards me and focused back in on his game.

"You and Sanaa ain't work out I see. Where the fuck you been at?" I looked this man in the face. He eventually looked towards me after excusing his lovely guest.

"Fuck you. You're a rapist. I know what you did. Don't speak to me in public nigga." Disgust coated his face as he brushed past me.

"I'm a what?!"

I stole off but Omar side stepped it, smoothly dippin my shit followed up with a powerful punch that knocked me square off my feet with immaculate precision. *Don't Worry Be Happy* was playing as I was in the air and on the ground within moments. A nigga saw stars, word up. After a few long humiliating seconds, a blur coated my vision as I looked around the casino and there she was. Clearly, Sole' Dubois reaching towards me with concern coating her face. *Prince baby get up! I'll kill him for hitting you! That big, jealous, goofy muthafukka! Get up baby!!!* I reached in the direction of a figment of my imagination towards dead air. A mirage. Blinking a few times, in actuality was Omar leaned over me.

"C'mon man. You did this to yourself. All this shit you're going through is self-inflicted. I quit."

Omar spat on the ground towards my feet, reached for his lady's arm and walked off. Lyle was standing there to my right.

"Prince! Yo you good? Why you and O beefin? Who you grabbing for man?"

Pushing past him, I gathered my shit and got the fuck outta there. I couldn't trust anybody. A single fuckin soul. Fury is an understatement. Bitch ass nigga called me a rapist and with conviction too! My lawyer was blowing up my line.

"What Frank."

"Twins Prince!! No Prince. Noo!!! Fuck did you do with them industry plant twins!"

I was frozen. The answer was nothing, I did nothing but fuck them. One at least. What Frank said next pushed me over the edge causing me to drop the phone to the ground.

The infamous night with the twins was simple. One twin was wit the shit and one wasn't which was whatever. The twin that was wit it was wit it so we were fucking all night. The corny twin recorded us while we partook in some wild roleplay. One role was burglar. All footage was allegedly deleted afterwards. Valentina was screaming while I pounded her out as she kept cummin and the shit was good but that's it. Consensual sex amongst adults. Never in a million years did I think they'd be using footage of me to ultimately blackmail me. The fact that Frank was insinuating there was audio of me raping a woman and potentially a video, broke my heart into a billion pieces. That shit hurt me to the core. Twenty million. The request.

I immediately called Bianca simply because I needed someone to be angry with. Needed someone to hate.

"Isn't it your responsibility to organize my bitches?"

"Umm…. yeah."

"The fuck is this twins bullshit?"

"What twins shit?"

"They're saying they're dropping a story about some rape shit if I don't pay em twenty million. Stop fuckin playing wit me!!"

"I organize your NDAs. You met them bitches at a bar."

"Fuck that. You're fired." *Bang!*

10

the root

Whe the lights get bright what's there
to do? What should I do? What's left
to do? No answers, just eerie silence.
Eerie silence until there isn't. Looking
around my mansion at all of my perceived freedom
caused me to just shut my eyes. Eyes shut; I see so much
darkness inside me so the only choice is to open them.
I'm safer with my eyes open. Mind in a haze, thirty
minutes past five and the sunrise would be here which
didn't matter because I'd been up all night. Fuck sleep at
this point. Eyelids heavy as shit, I felt better as daylight
would soon be here. Not as if daylight symbolized
anything. Just that I made it through the night. The fight
with Omar was fuckin with me and eleven million in the
hole was indeed heavy on my mental but my reputation
and integrity being tampered with was the straw that was
about to set everything off. I was hot off that shit. They
were really trying to hem me up and I didn't even trust
my attorney at this point. I sat back processing
everything. A room filled with dynamite fueled up
inside of me as I was close to blowing up. Ambling
towards my mirror to scope the damage, myself, I cut
my foot with some broken glass. The glass from when I
tossed Sole's drink on the ground before we had sex a
week ago, proving two things. Proof that housekeeping
wasn't cleaning thoroughly enough and that traces of
Sole' will always linger. Blood on the floor, I grabbed a
towel and eased the bleeding. Bandaged my toe and
continued my trip towards the mirror. Still me. Still
Prince. Fury was in my eyes obviously transmuted from
my heart. I was angry but deeper than that, in my eyes I

saw fear. I'd never seen fear in my eyes a day in my life. Even at nine when I bust my knee ultimately diminishing my hoop dreams, I still didn't see fear in my eyes. For the first time in a long time, I wished I could talk to my father. He'd know the exact thing to do in this moment. The right thing to say but he wasn't here so I just sat back down on the patio. Back into my dreary gaze. Destruction inflamed as this was true despair. Rock bottom. The hours. I was counting the hours at this point. Solitary confinement. I just needed to be still. If I kept still maybe I would just die already. Maybe I would begin to live. I just know there's power in stillness. Read that shit somewhere. I needed a masterplan; the blueprint and I wasn't moving until I found it. Wasn't leaving this seat. Around me displayed nothing but beauty. Inside me, the complete opposite.

Omar and my attorney Frank insinuating that I raped the twin was some heavy fuckin shit but I refused to let it take me out. Fuck them and them dirty lying bitches. The cryptic email requesting twenty million. They could suck my twenty-million-dollar dick. The actual eleven million I lost at the casino. I refused to think about that shit right now. Maria and her baby drama. The slut's clearly a fraud so we would let time tell with her, and my momma? *Damn ma.* Why did she of all people have to go through all this a second time? Why?! That was pulling at my heart strings for real. My heart couldn't delve into that right now either but I was praying for her deeply. My mom needed to be alright, and I'd see what the doctor was talking about next week.

Right now in this moment, I needed to save my own life. Get myself straight. *Fall in Love* by Phantogram simmered on low as I touched my cheek where Omar punched me, eventually applying ice to it. Couldn't even think too much on that either because the other half of my face felt numb which was terrifying and I wished I could tell someone of this metamorphosis, but no one would understand. Shit, I didn't understand as this was a rare thing. There was no diagnosis for this shit. I was all out of Adderall, but the weed was still around and I was officially losing my shit. A slow burn, I was crashing out bad. My demise was on simmer, a dream deferred. Only a billion prayers could cure me. A trillion. Looking towards my surveillance, I told myself not to watch the tape again but I did. Tears dripping from my face, I watched that shit and then I staggered back to my executive chair with all calls forwarded to Markell and Lyle. The night's tirades were too fucking heavy, so I called myself sleeping outside on my kabana and then I ended up collapsing to the floor. Probably due to running off fumes on the sleep tip for the last few years on top of the excess drinking. Working off weed and endless bottles of 1942, a big blur of bullshit yet in retrospect, I appreciated the rest. My gardener was watering the flowers, minding his fuckin business as I peeled myself off the ground and staggered inside. Sole' wasn't on social media and she was damn near impossible to track down so I had to swallow the truth. I'd probably never see her again. Only in a hyper dream and mind tirade would I see her and those are all distorted and wicked. Eyes shut tight; I had another one.

I let it happen and pushed through. Then I dropped to my to my knees and just stayed there for a while. I was doomed.

It was two days later when I got the epiphany, 7:15 on the dot. The only way to find Sole'. The only fuckin way. Couldn't believe I hadn't thought of this before. Hopping up, I grabbed the keys to my Maybach and was off across town towards the valley. Parked across the street in my unmarked car and then eventually strolled up towards the strip club she danced at. Paid my fee, got frisked and glazed inside skimming the perimeter immediately. *Where the fuck was she?* I didn't spot her immediately so I got a drink at the bar and made small talk with the bartender, keeping it low as that scandal with the twins had me feelin creepy as fuck out here.

"Why the bartenders always finer than the dancers?" I smiled slippin her a hundred-dollar bill.

"That's sweet." She grinned, slipping the money into her bra.

"Where's Sole'?" I got straight to the point and made myself comfortable.

"She only works once a month."

"I know. Where she at?" Eyes glued on shawty, I slipped her another hundred.

"We're not allowed to give out schedules and Queen Sole' doesn't have a schedule so your money wouldn't matter."

"I hear you." I slipped her one last hundred.

"Look. She pops up. Euphoric effect ya know. Enjoy your drink. Enjoy a show."

She pointed to the stage towards two beautiful women doing circus soleil tricks, swiveling around their respective poles. I wasn't here for that and this bitch was following protocol so I fell back. Stayed for a bit – no Sole'. I stumbled towards my whip and just stayed put until closing. Did the same thing the next night too. Night after that, except I stayed in the car. She'd be here eventually. Once a month. I was praying she hadn't come the day before I started my stalking spree because then I had a lot more of this shit to do.

It was happening again, a mind tirade. Grabbing my steering wheel, I closed my eyes tight, tears flowing. *Please God help me!* I breathed through it. This one lasted longer than normal. Pushing my driver seat back, I convulsed and threw up on myself. *Prince babyyyyy.* It was the voice of my wicked ex again! I simmered down as a swoosh of euphoria rushed through my body. Ignoring her and staying put and eventually I was back. Tossing my soiled tee out the window and changing, I pulled myself back together. I was a mess but fuck all that. Still parked across the street from the strip club, I was back to stalking. Lyle called me, probably about work but I sent him to voice mail. Not now. A few hours elapsed and no Sole' which was okay because I'd be there tomorrow. The next night too. Nine long, meaningless nights of nothing and I was on the brink of truly losing it.

It was night ten when I saw her. Dropped off in a black truck, there she was. Dressed in black sweatpants and a leather bra, fake ass femme fatale. Blinking my eyes to adjust, I mentally prepared myself to faceoff with my ex. Strolling in, I paid my fee and paid for a private dance. She was popular so she was booked up for a show and had her own dressing room exclusively upstairs. She came back out sporting an ice blue bob wig. Sparkles coated her face like a galaxy, a rhinestone g string graced her ass and heart pasties covered her nipples. She looked dumb. Madonna's *Human Nature* echoed through the spot and all eyes were on Sole'. Just like this bitch preferred. She spotted me mid-performance when she was upside down slithering down a pole by her clear heels, her face expressionless. Glossing the stage, she enticed the crowd working her magic. She kicked up a smidge after she spotted me. The crowd was mesmerized as she sprinkled her pixie dust on everybody and shit. I was so over this wicked bitch. In the spirit of never hating, she killed her performance as she always does but to keep it a buck, shawty who went after her did better. Sole' was evil and I'm not into poisonous pussy. I don't support it. Whatever the fuck she did to me, she was reversing that shit tonight! I took back a drink and six minutes later I was following her into the very expensive champagne room.

"You look beautiful."

"...and you look like shit."

"That's how you treat all your customers?" I took a seat, eyes glued to this deceitful monster.

"Only the narcissist stalkers."

"What...did...you...do...to...me?"

She rolled her eyes, preparing for her dance. Swaying to the melodies, ignoring my disdain, my pain, my torturous days and nights, my weary she seemed so oblivious.

"Sole'."

"All I did was make the decision to leave you alone."

"Oh yeah? You a klepto now?"

"Oh don't pretend like you miss the painting."

"This isn't about a fuckin painting!!"

"Don't curse at me." She pointed towards the eyes in the ceiling, then began to sway to the music.

"This isn't about that. This is about my mind Sole'. I'm not well, can't you fuckin tell? I love you. Always have and I don't want problems with you. Never have. I've been going through it. Bad. Real bad. Look at me!"

She finally looked towards me.

"I don't know what to do anymore." I poured my heart at her feet, tears dripping from my eyes as she stared at me.

"No. No this is about your ego. I chose to be with Mike, someone who doesn't nitpick at every little thing I do and you're having a tantrum about it. I can't play the violin for you. You're used to people needing you for survival or at least appearing to but that's not even the main thing. The main thing is you know *I* of all people *earned* that painting."

"You earned dick you slut bitch!!!"

Sole' just grew quiet, obviously taken back as I'd never spoken to her like that before.

"You're making me uncomfortable."

"You're a ghetto girl from the muddy bayou and I'm a dirty project nigga from Yonkers. I'm not making you feel a thing. I *need* to talk to you." I emphasized in her direction.

"You've made that clear." She pulled out a joint and sighed deeply as it was quiet for a moment. "We can meet at Calvin's tomorrow at three and Prince, this meeting will be our last conversation."

"You know what I just realized? I'm a sick nigga to not think this shit was convoluted back then. A grown woman in a monogamous relationship touching her toes for strangers. Where's the queen in that right? Whatever you did to me, it's cool. It's ight. One thing for sure, i'ma get that ass. I always do."

"You want your dance or nah? You paid a thousand dollars." She was ignoring my shit and her eyes were cold. I hurt her feelings but fuck her feelings.

"Keep the band, you obviously need it more than I do and last time I let you dance for me..........I ended up, here. You look beautiful." Standing to my feet, I walked out of the champagne room towards my car. Grabbed a blunt, lit that shit and put on some Stevie Wonder for the ride home.

The next day I met Sole' at Calvins at the requested time. Tossing back water, I was too livid to eat. Two hours had to elapse for me to grasp the fact that she was standing me up. Two fuckin hours. Power walking to my whip, I rushed towards the strip club to get back to my stalking. Back to the creep shit. Sole' had me fucked up, clearly. Two additional nights of stalking, I opted to go in and ask for Sole'.

"Sole' quit baby. Permanently."

The country bartender popped her gum while she served her customers. Had I heard her correctly? Sole' quit? I sat there for a minute which turned into the remainder of the night. Got a couple of comatose lap dances and did the walk of shame back to my truck and finally went home. She won.

The next day I called my sis Wanda and it didn't go through. She had apparently changed her number. Reached out to a few of my other industry friends and the energy was just off. Was I being blackballed? It was still business as usual, so I was pushing myself. Paid my eleven-million-dollar debt by selling a couple things, moving a few things around and that was that. I was working around the mind tirades at this point. Lyle came through one rainy night blasting his music on the pullup.

"Prince! Open the door!"

He yelled obnoxiously. Once he was in we talked about the fight with Omar and then I told him a little bit about my ex-girlfriend. Lyle was young and wild but he was solid and he deserved transparency.

"That's wild pressure my boy."

"Tell me about it."

"You heard of the story of Cersei?"

"Nah."

"She was a sorceress and a minor goddess known for her vast knowledge of potions and herbs. The daughter of Helios the sun god and of the ocean nymph Perse. She was able by means of drugs and incantations to change humans into wolves, lions and swine my nigga. The Greek hero Odysseus visited her island with his friends and she turned them muthafukkas into swine. That's ya ho."

"Lyle, nigga is you high?" I looked towards my boy.

"Hell yeah. Did a shroom before I got here but that don't mean shit. I'm tapped in. She was turning niggas into swine Prince. Coined the phrase *men are pigs*. Stay woke. Protect ya neck."

"Fuck both them toxic bitches."

"You say she from New Orleans?"

"Pretty much."

"Them creole girls know that voodoo. Nigga I'm going home. You probably got a root on you." Lyle grabbed his keys. "Be at work tomorrow and take a spiritual bath or something. Don't come into the office with that monkey on ya back."

"Lyle take ya high ass home and text me when you get in."

I laughed at my boy, watching him stumble down the driveway. He drove his Tesla so he was safe. House to the face, I appreciated Lyle's energy. My mom's appointment was tomorrow so I focused in on that. The next morning I received a call from Akon himself asking to meet him for some legitimate business. Claimed he was a big fan of my story and had a twelve-million-dollar deal on display. Immediate dough. I had to meet him at noon which was cool because mom's appointment was at three. Zooming towards the lucrative deal, my hands gripped the steering wheel. Pulling up momentarily, I awaited Akon. I always wanted to do business with him so I was lowkey excited as shit. One pm is when he texted me stating he'd be there in twenty minutes. Palms sweaty with my eyes glued to the time, I played it cool. I needed to leave here in thirty minutes to meet my mom. No biggie. Fifteen minutes later I called Akon again as he was in LA traffic but close so I just buckled and called my mom.

"Ma. Can Aunt Kelly go with you? I've got…."

"Prince Roberson! No, *you* come with me." My mom demanded.

"I'll send yall a nice car and then to a nice lunch and wherever you want ma. Shopping, spas. Name it, you got it. Please just understand this one time! I beg of you."

My mom was quiet. "Okay."

"Thank you. I'll send the car."

"No your aunt can grab me. Handle your business son." She hung up while Akon was pulling up, except it wasn't Akon. It was some light skinned brotha.

"My bad. Akon needed to reschedule. Family shit. Here's a hundred bands for your time. He'll reach out."

A knot was thrown into my whip as I sat there astounded. Calling my mother back, her call went to voice mail. Thirty more calls and nothing. I dropped to my knees and prayed for her, then and there. An anonymous text popped up on my screen. *The money or the tape.* Teeth clenched, I rushed home doing God knows how fast. Before I knew it the airbags were busting towards my chest and face. Peeping the environment, my whip merged into a tree and glass was scattered all over. To the left, Sole' standing at the bus stop. Blinked again and she disappeared. Fleeing the scene, I limped away and called a taxi home. I don't know why I left but I did. Scratches across my face and ribs a bit bruised, I pushed the fuck on. Once arrived, I slammed the door as tears drenched my face. Heading to my bedroom my eyes darted towards a polaroid of Ashley and I at the pier. Drying my tears as that picture made me smile, I walked closer towards it noticing something was off. My smile converted into confusion as something wasn't quite right. Snatching it off my nightstand, I zoomed in. In place of Ashley there she was. Sole' herself. Sole' was in place of my sweetheart Ashley! Balling up the photo, I stormed downstairs to my fireplace and tossed the picture into the flames. Not today. Not fuckin today. Running through my mansion on the brink of a meltdown, there she was again. This time hidden in a piece of art containing thirteen African people dancing. Sole' was front and center, a red dress on her body, a flower in her mouth. Darting back upstairs, plastered across my television displayed the name Sole' Peters. Symptoms of her everywhere. I grabbed the nearest object and broke my television. Swiped everything off my walls and tables. Yeah, I was losing it and I couldn't stop. Trashing my spot, I went apeshit. Tossing clothes all over the place, objects and devices, I ensured I knocked everything off every single wall. I now stood in front of my million-dollar mirror eyes closed. I was afraid to open my own fuckin eyes! Once I opened them, I stared into my reflection and way deep in the pupils of my dilated eyeballs was *her*. The bitch! Man, fuck this place. Banging my fist through the mirror, I began breaking every mirror in my mansion.

The rampage of a madman. No room was safe. Panting wildly, I awaited the next wave. The next attack. The next hyper dream. The next mind tirade. The next. The next. The....I collapsed to the ground and there was nothing left to say.

When I awoke, Markell, Lydia, my two housekeepers Rachel and Mahalia, and a local medic was standing over me.

"Thank God!"

My housekeeper gasped as I blinked, adjusting to my environment. Sitting up, Markell handed me a cup of tea as the others dispersed. I looked towards my phone to another anonymous text. *The twenty million, you have two days.*

"Markell. Respectfully, clear my home out." I requested with my eyes shut.

"They already leaving bro and they signed their NDAs. I'm staying here until you get better. We ain't gotta talk about shit. Let's just chill."

Markell reached for the remote and grabbed a menu to order food. I just stayed put. My home was clean thanks to my staff. Walls bare as shit but it was clean. The clock read eleven o'clock. Laying on the floor, I kept my eyes closed. Markell tossed me some blankets and lay on a nearby sofa.

"I'm not here because you crashed the car and trashed your mansion like a fuckin rockstar and shit. It's your shit, fuck it up. Not here because I've been having to act as your PR, putting out mini fires because you won't express what's really going on wit you and won't communicate. No judgment to all of that. I'm here because I spoke to your Aunt Kelly."

"What's up with ma?!?" My heart was beating like a wild drummer attempting to burst out my chest.

"She's okay. Just mad at you. She and Aunt Kelly are in Hawaii on vacation. She'll reach out to you soon. She loves you, just mad at ya."

I exhaled deep, grateful that my mom was okay. All I needed to hear.

"Bruce is in the ICU."

"Fuck Bruce."

"You fired Bianca?"

"Fuck her too."

"Say less."

All in My Head by Sir sifted through the mansion which is stripped bare at this point. Flashes of me fucking up my multimillion-dollar spot floated through my head. A fuckin mad man. The next day I finally made it up to my room and got some well needed rest. I woke up with misery still festering in my heart. Markell was kicked back on the computer orchestrating some Prince Apparel shit when I walked into the living room. Out on my balcony, there she was. I stood there, stone faced. No rapid sweating, no tripping out. Sole' was standing out on the balcony in a sheer robe, naked, looking off into the LA stratosphere. I ignored her because it wasn't her, it was my mind. Laying on my sofa, I ignored the mirage of my ex and closed my eyes. Looked back towards the balcony and she was gone. Back towards Markell who was staring at me.

"You know I love you bro and I'd never call you crazy. Never...."

I took back some water and sat up. "What's up."

"Your mind right bro? What's really going on wit you?"

Ignoring my best friend, I strolled towards the bar and made a drink. Markell wrapped up his meeting and kicked back.

"Roll up."

"I never say this but I'm all out. Waiting for a drop off but fuck all that. What's up man?"

"Stop asking that shit."

I rolled up a roach blunt as I told myself to stay out my head.

"Fuck LA."

"Shut up Prince. You made ya millions in LA."

"Lost my fuckin mind in LA too."

"Technically you lost ya mind *in* Sole'."

"I don't wanna hear that shit right now. Fuck LA."

"I hear you."

"Nah for real, fuck em. Fake ass city. New York is hard on the body but LA is hard on the soul. The eerie complacency. Everything is transactional. Action enterprise relationships bullshit. We lost our grip a long time ago. The human experience is flawed and polluted. Surrounded by fucking blood suckers yo. Soul erosions. Everyone only gives a fuck about their own bottom line. Disingenuous bullshit muthafukkas. Fuck LA."

"Nigga. You saying all that with an NWA tee shirt on. Stop it." Markell laughed as I passed him the joint.

"I'm serious man. All this take a meeting to take a meeting phony shit. The facades and optics. Fuck that. I'm too raw for this shit. You too raw for this shit too."

"Well, my wife loves the sunshine out here so."

Weed was dropped off along with some Peruvian food and we kicked back like frat kids. Day three of bullshittin in the mansion with Markell, I was now kicked up on the couch as Markell smoked a blunt on the balcony. I had acquired ten mental tirades, one hyper dream and was working off six hours of sleep. I'd see her but I'd pretend like I didn't because I didn't want to sound crazy in front of my best friend. Worry sifted from Markell but he hid it well. He just wanted me to get right. Get better. Tea, video games, meditation, working out, vent sessions, basketball, games of pool, the whole third season of The Wire – Markell was trying and he never judged. Ever. It was around four o'clock when he said the dumbest shit he'd said in a long time though. He was out on the balcony and I was kicked up with a wash cloth draped over my eyes, cooling down from another one.

"Maybe you should just marry the bitch."

"The fuck?!"

"You heard me. Can't stop thinking about her. Plaguing ya fuckin mind. I seen yall two happy together eons ago, once upon a time. Vague but I saw it.

Anything beats this shit you goin through. If I couldn't stop thinking about a woman, I'd lock her down. Shit can't beat em, join em."

"Pass the fuckin weed Markell."

Three blunts later and some Chinese, I was lay out in fetal position on the floor. I hadn't had a vision in a few hours and I felt a swoosh of peace so I guess you can say I was basking in that. Relishing in tranquility. I just didn't want to move. It was three hours away from the alleged *rape tape* release and I was trying to avoid thinking about it whatsoever. If I thought about it ain't no telling what I'd do. Shit too heavy. Murky fuckin waters. If that tape leaked, my innocence wouldn't even matter. I'd be finished so I stayed put on the floor. Maybe if I kept still, I'd be back to me. The real me. The true me. My real life.

"This looks just like ya shit." Markell blurted as he was buried in his laptop.

"What shit?"

"Your shit."

"Who's shit?"

"Your Basquiat."

Hopping to my feet, I darted towards Markell's computer screen. Someone was selling a Basquiat and it looked like mine.

"That's my shit." Eyes barging out my head, I paced the room like a madman.

"Calm down nigga. It may not be yours."

"That's my shit," I reiterated.

"She ain't dumb enough to be selling a Basquiat that she stole from you on black market. Nah. Call Lyle to confirm. Don't get yaself worked up for nothing."

An hour later Lyle was at my spot confirming what I already knew. I left my team in my home, grabbed my jacket and keys and dipped out. They could let themselves out. I went to the barbershop and got a cut. Mid-cut my phone is ringing and it's my attorney screaming turn on the tv! Plastered across channel 5, the industry twin scammer sluts were arrested for fraud, embezzlement and a whole list of other shit. A list of men they attempted to scam for millions scrolled across the screen, forth in line being yours truly in a navy pinstriped suit. Good photo. I was scott free! After my haircut and victory, I rode to my headquarters and took a shower. Then I tossed on some classic all white linen. No shirt. Hopped back in my droptop and emailed Sole' from an anonymous John Doe email posing as a potential buyer. She emailed me back quick too. Sent her an address and then I drove towards my yacht. Coasting up the highway, laser focused with anticipation. Sole' always used to claim that I never knew the right things to say but magically at this very moment, I knew what she meant. *I get it now baby.* Driving a little too fast, a little too caught up in my head, I hit the brakes preventing an accident. Horns beeping wildly mixed with a few curses, the car in front of me was back on course. Across their bumper sticker read *Love Is The Only Way.* Two red lights later I decided to give everyone in my company Christmas bonuses – something I'd never done. It was September but fuck it. A few clicks from my phone and the money was dispersed. That felt good. The new Prince. I was in a good space and I hadn't felt like this in years. Finally pulling up to my yacht Yoruba, it was time.

11

(untitled) how does it feel

It was me, Bruce, my mom and dad, exactly one month before I hurt my knee. Dancing in the living room to the *Big Pay Back*. My dad had just won some money, seven hundred dollars. We'd later learn he robbed a corner boy for it. A corner boy who happened to be the son of a heavy hitter. He wasn't a nobody. Anyway, that night we were dancing and celebrating. My mom had just finished grading papers and cooking as Bruce and I took turns completing our chores. Now we were dancing. Coney Island was the promise. We were going to go to Coney Island and then Disneyland. My dad was going to buy my mom a real nice dress too. That was the dream. My mom was off to the market the next day to get some stuff for dinner when they barged into our apartment. Now, today I sit here with tears in my eyes putting it all behind me. All of it.

Glazing up towards my yacht, the wind felt perfect against my linen threads and skin. I wiped my tears as I strolled in, everything feeling like it was slow motion. Like a movie. Maybe it was the Soma and Lexapro. Maybe it was something deeper. More spiritual. I looked towards my watch ensuring I was prompt for my special guest. Strolling past the glowing onyx wet bar towards the master suite, I took a look around me. Rare Asian wood coated the walls crafted to replicate ripples of the ocean. The cream, soft furnishes and crisp structures and plunge tub with the Japanese waterspout. Italian leather plush sofas with rich art peppered all-around. Hopping up the bubinga wooden steps towards my captain's quarters, I took a look at myself in a small nearby mirror. No fear in my eyes. None at all. Heading back to the cockpit, I strolled over towards my favorite chair that looked off into the ocean and took a seat. A smile coated my face, a juxtaposition to my team's theories and for a moment I missed the quintet. The guys. Brief, super brief. Tonight was about Sole' only, not Prince Apparel. I sent Sole' a follow-up text as she was ten minutes away. On a nearby table lay one bottle of champagne and a fruit spread – simplicity. Now we wait. Death to *Mr So What*. It was quiet and the yacht was steady. It'd been nineteen hours since I had a mind tirade or hyper dream. Nineteen hours to be exact. Was I anxious? Nah. I was ready. Sole' always said I wasn't the romantic type. She always knew I had it in me though. I'm ready now. She always said I never knew the right things to say. I know now. Three minutes later I hear high heels as she was here. Standing to my feet, I awaited Sole' Dubois with my head high. A white flowy wrap dress graced her perfect body. A simple long ponytail dripped down her back. She noticed me and hesitated, followed up with a baby pure gasp. After ten seconds of being stunned, she finished walking towards me.

"I should've known it was you. You want your painting back that bad? You can have it. I'm exhausted at this point." She got straight to talkin her shit like she always does.

"I want you to have the painting. I should've given it to you."

She was quiet. Stunned again, eyes wide as for once she had nothing to say. I pointed towards the circular table for us to share a meal. Pulling out her chair she finally obliged and took a seat.

"I don't give a fuck about that art shit. That's your thing."

"I hear you. You still think I cursed you? You still stickin to that?"

"No."

"You're the most selfish person I've ever met."

"Yeah I hear you baby. Why you selling my painting?"

Sole rolled her eyes and whipped out a blunt in defeat, inhaling deep before blowing smoke from her lips. Heart-shaped smoke circles floated through the air as she looked towards me and then out into the ocean.

"I need the money. Broke it off with Mike. Wanted to open up a photography slash dance studio."

I watched her smoke until her eyes got low. Pulled out my own weed and we smoked in silence while we watched the sun set. Just the ocean and our breathing. So much was said in that silence.

"How can someone suffer so much emotionally but still be so in love on a whole different existence and time?"

"Because love always conquers all. Love knows no logic. Love does what it wants."

"Keep the painting. Don't sell it. You'd never forgive yourself for it."

Sole' grew quiet, sipping her wine and picking at her fruit. We listened to the ocean for a good minute.

"You're the only man I've ever loved."

"I'm sorry for every sunset and sunrise I missed when we were apart." I looked towards Sole' who now had tears dripping from her eyes.

"They're priceless."

"I know that now. All you ever wanted was to spend every sunset and sunrise with me. I get it baby."

"I always felt that…" She hesitated. "Always felt that if I had that with you, no matter how big and famous you got or how distracting Hollywood became for us we would always have priceless art together, you and me. Every sunset and sunrise is a moment of art. You don't even have to create it, it just *is* and though maybe I couldn't give you babies, I could make priceless memories with you. When I mentioned it to you in college, you acted like me wanting all your sunrises and sunsets was me sending you to the electric chair or something."

"Wait, hold up. You don't know what the universe had in store for us when it came to us starting a family."

"Just forget I brought it up."

Sole' had suffered two miscarriages back-to-back in the past and it traumatized her. Shit, me too. I was young and naïve and not an emotionally supportive partner back then, I'll own that. After she had the first one, I bought her a designer bag for comfort and after the second, took her to the fuckin opera and spa. We never even talked about it, I just wanted to keep trying. It's fun trying. She hopped on birth control and we just kept fuckin. The way I handled it was whack back then in retrospect, but I didn't know better. We were young. A swoosh of creative expansion filled me as I felt more connected to this queen. I couldn't go backwards but I could push forward for sure. I gave her a forehead kiss and we sipped champagne and ate fruit and then we slow danced to the sounds of the ocean. We never needed music. Sole' melted into my arms and we danced barefoot, all white what a sight. Black love. The real shit.

"I torpedoed my entire world for you Prince, and what do you offer me in return? A job."

"I wanted you to be my partner."

"In exchange for a fuck under the California sun?"

"You could always have whatever you wanted from me. You know that."

Sole' wiped her tear-streaked cheeks. "Our love is too complicated."

I just pulled her closer to me and kept dancing under the moonlight. Maybe we're better misunderstood. I knew she was just afraid. Afraid to surrender fully, I get it. Nothing a little nurturing and time couldn't remedy. Consistency. Love. I understood her fully for the first time in our dynamic. We reminisced a lil.

"I saw the news. They threw away your cases."

"Yup."

"You're blessed. God's favorite."

"I am. Are you still hungry? I can have my chef whip up something."

"The fruit is fine. Thank you."

"Ok." I kissed her manicured hand.

"You surprise me Prince. I have never seen this side of you."

I just gave her a wink while refilling her champagne flute. Sitting back, watching her beautiful ass enjoy her fruit.

"What you looking at?"

"Priceless art." I grabbed her drink to take a sip.

"Don't you have your own glass *big money*?" She interjected grabbing her drink from my grip.

"You didn't have a problem with me sipping from your glass all them times in college, sippin on that cheap ass Arbor Mist and Paul Masson... or that time we shared endless glasses of wine in Italy... and at the vineyard or the time we'd sip Henny straight out the bottle visiting my mom in the projects in New York... or when I sipped that expensive ass champagne off your pretty body in Tahiti that one time."

"You know what Prince? We have come a very long way."

Sole' let out a giggle that made her dimples stand out more. Hopping to her feet, she began walking up on me before tilting my head back slightly and pouring a lil champagne into my mouth. Before I could swallow it she slurped it up like a shot, ensuring to get all the remnants up. Shit we used to do in college. Our tongues danced momentarily as we shared a brief but deep kiss. I traced my fingertips across her legs as she fed me a strawberry and then she was back in her seat. Sole', champagne and fruit lingered in my mouth - tastes of Heaven, the perfect trifecta.

"Yes, I have come along way."

"Pardon?"

"You've always been lightyears ahead of me. Shit, I'm finally catching up to you."

"What you talkin about?"

"What you mean what am I talkin about?"

"What are you sayin?"

"You know you've always danced circles around me girl. I used to love to watch you do it too."

She just smiled as we smoked a few more blunts and enjoyed each other's company.

"I guess a part of me knew you'd come looking for me if I took the painting. You always find me. Always. I knew my taking your shit would bring you to your senses."

"Oh yeah?"

"Yeah. I know you better than anyone. I know you better than your own momma."

"Negative." We both just laughed.

"No for real. No one knows you better than me. I'm the one who sat there when you were broke, days and nights and days and nights trying to get this high-end suit line off the ground. I was your muse for years. Trust me, I know you baby."

"You're so fuckin pretty."

"Thank you but Prince, you're not gonna give me an elaborate tour of your yacht like you did ya mansion?"

"Nah."

"Why not?"

"Because you only give a fuck about the view and the moment. You don't care about my yacht or anything material unless it's art and you already have my best piece of art. Sitting right here with you is fine with me."

Sole' sat back with her eyebrows raised, clearly impressed. Shit, I was impressing myself with this new ascended version of me. Sole' reapplied her lipstick keeping her eyes on me.

"Gimme a tour of your yacht."

"Nah. *You* give me a tour of *my* yacht."

I hopped up and grabbed her hand as I instructed her to lead the way. She stumbled aimlessly towards the direction of my board meeting room first, pretending to be a sexy tour guide.

"This is where King Prince handles all his business, taking all the people's moneyyyyy. Extorting from the rich and giving to the poor is his motto. *Black Robin Hood* style and no, the rumors aren't true. There was never a Ponzi scheme honey." Sole' winked as she crawled across my long table, dramatically spewing sarcasm and giggles.

"Awww." I touched my heart pretending to be offended, a huge grin on my face.

"Next room!" Sole' hopped up, skipping around my yacht towards my master suite.

"This is where King Prince makes all his loveeeee. It happens so frequent, and the king is so busy that he doesn't even have time to name his bitches. What do you call em again? Jane Hos?"

"Jane Does." I laughed out loud.

"Yeah that's what I said. By the way, King Prince never met them twinssss." Sole' smiled twirling around like DeeDee from Dexter's Laboratory. She had jokes.

"Cute."

"I'm just being silly baby. No really, give me a real tour." She wined, snuggling up close to me. I showed her around a bit, switching up the pace and she seemed relaxed and amazed.

"It's so beautiful Prince."

"Thank you."

"No like, wow."

I watched her admire my yacht and everyone knows how I love watching Sole' love something.

"So Miss Dubois, what's your favorite part about us?"

"Us?"

"You heard me."

"Well, Mister Roberson... I always feel free with you. Safe and free. Unexplainable. I can't find that anywhere else."

Sole' untied her hair clip allowing her hair to fall free as I loved her answer. She didn't have to ask me the same question. She knew I loved everything about her. Leading her towards my captains' quarters to chill, everything feelng slow motion again. Sole' tossed on a nearby sailor hat, prancing around as she fucked with the gadgets of the ship. So beautiful, like a Sports Illustrated model and shit. We chopped it up like homies and I even ran a few business plans by her. Detail by detail.

"That's dope. That's your billion-dollar shit right there."

"You think so?"

"I know it."

Every time Sole' said shit like that, she was always right. Always. She always pushed me and painted the picture out for me and I always exceeded it. *Trippy* by Anderson Paak and J Cole sifted through the room while we twisted up one last blunt and smoked. A jumbo lazy boy sat nearby and Sole' lay out on it. I was on her ass but she pushed me away sweetly – cat and mouse shit. I massaged her feet as I kept my eyes on her, eventually feeling her energy intensify a smidge.

"Take them clothes off." She bit her lip seductively.

"Relax. I got you."

Surveying the room, I spot some roses and a small flowerpot on a nearby mantle. Walking towards it, I grabbed it while my muse's back was turned. Tracing her body with the petals, I started with her lips. Sole' attempted to grab the rose at a point but I slid her control freak lil hands off it. It was my way tonight.

"You trust me?"

"I do."

That was my cue so I tied her wrists up lightly so I could really blow her beautiful mind. She let me because she's freaky like that. I circled her pretty ass like a shark before tracing her body with the petals again.

"Simplicity. One rose is true romance right? Never a dozen. Just one."

She smiled my way while I talked that sexy shit in her ears as she tried not to squirm. Her fragrance, enchanting and alluring as always. I traced the rose from her crotch up her body making her quiver, then up and down her thighs. Up and down, round and round. Once I heard her moan, I knew I had her. That's when I knew. She was mine. Thoughts of the nine-carat diamond ring in my pocket flashed through my mind for a moment which made me smile. Plans on whipping it out during tomorrow's sunrise lingered. Would be the biggest day of my life and God willing she'd say *yes*. Suddenly, every hyper dream and mental tirade I had ever encountered rolodexed through my brain at once, like a staticky broken television. Lightning waves zigzagged through my mind in waves and you can say I short circuited. Yeah, that's what I'd call it. A short-circuit. Wrapping the thorny vine around her pretty neck, I strangled her with all my might. Blood splattered all over my white linen and her white dress as I'd obviously ruptured her artery. Eyes shut tight, I pulled at both ends of the vine as if I was tying a shoelace real tight. Illusions unmasked and the death was quick. Standing to my feet, I ambled towards the sink and washed my hands. For some reason I wasn't trippin about the cleanup. Wasn't trippin bout shit. Didn't even look back at her. I'm sure it was a beautiful mess. The water coated my hands as a pool of blood filled my sink. Endless blood. One rose pedal lay near my shoe.

Looking down towards my fingertips, what was done was done. I kept my head down as the water trickled amidst my fingertips while I stood in front of my sink and mirror. Eventually the sink water was clear again, symptoms of clean hands. Cupping my hands under the faucet, I let the water overflow before splashing some on my face, removing excess blood. Reaching for a towel, I wiped off my face as well as my transgressions. Mind a bit warped yet this was justice. The only way. *Goodbye Sole'. Bye baby.* A smirk alongside a swoosh of serenity coated my spirit as I finally conjured up the courage to look up at myself in the mirror into my reflection. The setting was off though as I was no longer in my captain's quarters anymore but in my master suite. Confusion coated my face as I stood tall in front of my graffiti textured accent mirror, the one with the crack in the corner. No blood. No rose. No traces of Sole'. *Prince don't trip* is what I told myself as the kaleidoscope of experiences permeated my mental. Straightening my tie and fixing the lapel to my perfectly color blocked suit, I stood there. Over my shoulder in my reflection, my hired guest. A little black dress draped her body, Dior stilettos graced her feet. Pink lipstick stains coated her champagne flute, remnants of sushi and oysters alongside some Mr Chow and McCallan 18. A bottle of 1942 sat empty on a nearby table. I noticed she resembled my ex, only finer. Clearly tonight's Jane Doe. *Between the Sheets* by the Isley Brothers serenaded the master suite and I could hear a party happening outside the door. A *Happy Birthday Prince* banner hung above me, symptoms of a celebration. I read the room attempting not to internally unravel. A million moments ricocheted through my mind as I couldn't correlate the sequence of events of my life. Nothing made sense. This didn't make sense. I didn't make sense. What….the….fuck! My heart began pounding out my chest like a fuckin wild drummer and beads of sweat started brewing. Looking towards my guest in despair as her slanted eyes was still glued on yours truly, she recrossed her legs seductively, a glimmer of sincerity in her eyes. She perched her lips up and asked me…

"What are you thinkin about?"

Made in the USA
Monee, IL
19 July 2022